PRAISE FOR

WINNER
Governor General's Literary Award for
French-Language Fiction
Prix littéraire France-Québec
Prix Ringuet
Prix littéraire des collégiens

"There are four hundred times more descriptions of snow than you'd find in the average novel, yet that is precisely the right amount."
—*New York Magazine*

"A book that shines like snow melting under a winter sun."
—Josée Lapointe, *La Presse*

"It's not easy to make such a simple story both profound and compulsively readable, but Guay-Poliquin pulls it off in this literary page-turner."
—*Montreal Review of Books*

PRAISE FOR RUNNING ON FUMES

"A taut story of mental and civil collapse."
—*Globe and Mail*

"Brilliant and well-mastered writing."
—*La Presse*

"*Running on Fumes* is a Canadian legend processed as Canadian mythology."
—*Prairie Fire*

ALSO BY
CHRISTIAN GUAY-POLIQUIN

Running on Fumes
Translated by Jacob Homel

The Weight of Snow
Translated by David Homel

Published by Talonbooks

FALLING SHADOWS

CHRISTIAN GUAY-POLIQUIN

TRANSLATED BY DAVID HOMEL

TALONBOOKS

© 2021 Christian Guay-Poliquin
© 2021 Éditions La Peuplade
Translation © 2022 David Homel

All rights reserved. No part of this book may be reproduced, stored in a retrieval system, or transmitted, in any form or by any means, without the prior written consent of the publisher or a licence from Access Copyright (the Canadian Copyright Licensing Agency). For a copyright licence, visit accesscopyright.ca or call toll-free 1-800-893-5777.

Talonbooks
9259 Shaughnessy Street, Vancouver, British Columbia, Canada v6p 6r4
talonbooks.com

Talonbooks is located on xʷməθkʷəy̓əm, Sḵwx̱wú7mesh, and səl̓ilwətaʔɬ Lands.

First printing: 2022

Typeset in Sabon
Printed and bound in Canada on 100% post-consumer recycled paper
Interior and cover design by Typesmith
Cover illustration by Stéphane Poirier

Talonbooks acknowledges the financial support of the Canada Council for the Arts, the Government of Canada through the Canada Book Fund, and the Province of British Columbia through the British Columbia Arts Council and the Book Publishing Tax Credit.

This work was originally published in French as *Les ombres filantes* by Éditions La Peuplade, Saguenay, Québec, in 2021. We acknowledge the financial support of the Government of Canada through the National Translation Program for Book Publishing, an initiative of the *Roadmap for Canada's Official Languages 2013–2018: Education, Immigration, Communities*, for our translation activities.

Library and Archives Canada Cataloguing in Publication

Title: Falling shadows / Christian Guay-Poliquin ; translated by David Homel.
Names: Guay-Poliquin, Christian, 1982– author. | Homel, David, translator.
Description: Translation of: Les Ombres filantes.
Identifiers: Canadiana 20220217904 | ISBN 9781772014518 (softcover)
Classification: LCC PS8613.U297 O4313 2022 | DDC C843/.6—dc23

For Huguette
and all her family

Here is the door, here is the open air.
—ROBERT LOUIS STEVENSON
"The Lantern-Bearers" (1888)

I.	FOREST	3
II.	FAMILY	97
III.	SKY	209

ACKNOWLEDGMENTS 244

It is the beginning and the end. It was there before anyone could see it, and it will be there after sight has gone. It is the epicentre, the knot, the refuge, the cell. It fascinates and fills us with dread. Under its cloak, encounters are few and decisive. Time is its life force. Its disorder enchants, its shadows merge, its murmur is heard from all sides. It is the opposite of anything that thinks. It is instinct, act, recoil. All souls dream of losing themselves in it. But no living thing emerges unscathed from its embrace. It is the simplest, most complete, most opaque solution to the calculation of unquiet hearts.

FOREST

AFTERNOON

Something pulls me from sleep. I will not open my eyes. Not yet, not right now. I don't know how long I managed to doze with my back against this old stump. An hour, maybe two. Besides a crow cawing in the distance and the poplar leaves whispering in the wind, the forest is silent.

I open my eyelids. Ferns numerous, slender, and luminescent dazzle me. In the endless space, giant trees make a grab for the sky. The rough bark of their trunks is covered with lichen. The labyrinth of their branches cuts the vegetation into a green mosaic.

A smell of wild animal hangs in the air. I lift my head and shiver. In front of me, right close by, just there, a wolf is watching me. Its yellow eyes, its size, its shadowy coat belong to another world. I want to get up and move away, but the bones of my spine have been welded together. I have never seen an animal so still yet so powerful.

When I manage to get to my feet, the wolf backs off a few steps, sizes me up, then returns to its position. The old injury to my knee sends up a pain signal. I look over my shoulder. Between the brown and tawny branches, I spot two other shapes in silent movement. My blood freezes. I am surrounded. Either they are about to leap at me, or they think my skinny, fleshless body isn't worth the effort. I shout to try and frighten them. My voice breaks. The wolf in front of me is surprised, then waits and raises its muzzle to sniff the air. I keep my eyes on it as I lean over and reach for my bag, my sticks, my old boots.

I retreat slowly, very slowly, barefoot in the dead leaves. A few steps and the animals are invisible behind the crisscross of branches and underbrush. I start running through the forest. Twigs snap beneath my weight and jab the soles of my feet. I bog down in the brush, stumble, nearly fall over a root. A sharp pain jolts my damaged knee. I grit my teeth and limp over to a ridge and try to hide behind it the best I can, gasping for air, sweating. I look around. I am disoriented. The forest grows denser. Shadows rise up. My heart pounds. Every bush hides a piercing pair of eyes, a furtive movement, a trap.

I keep watch for a while, tormented by my imagination. As my thoughts grow calmer, I catch my breath. I shake myself, and with trembling hands, put my boots back on as if I were never going to take them off again.

MIDDAY

My hips crack. My toes cramp up. The straps of my pack dig into my shoulders. My knee is a constant source of pain. But the body is a formidable machine. Every day, I take hold of my sticks and move under verdant domes, I cross streams and step over fallen trees. Every day, I move a little deeper into this network of galleries, veins, and topography. And try to avoid encounters.

This morning, I have been following a twisting path made by animals. The rocks jut out, the roots form thick knots, my pack is heavy and cumbersome. I move forward the best I can, one step at a time, with the stubborn gait of a labouring beast.

When the sun stands straight above my head and my stomach grumbles, I stop for a break at the top of some higher ground. I snack on a handful of dried fruit and try to figure out how long I have been gone. Ten days? Twelve? Time is slipping away. The scene changes. Distances dilate. I look around. Below lies a clearing. I sling my pack back onto my shoulders, reach the clearing, and come upon a dirt road.

I had better be careful. Blackflies buzz around my head. In one direction, the road moves up the side of a mountain. In the other, it heads downward and disappears around a bend. I take a drink of water and the beating wings of a pheasant startle me. I take a few steps sideways and emerge from the cover of the trees.

My eyes get used to the sudden brightness as the sun beats down on the back of my neck. The air is hot and dry. Stones roll under the soles of my boots. My footsteps echo off the green walls of the forest. Here and there, grass has crawled down and taken over the edge of the road. Deep ruts have been drawn in it by the rain and melting snow. The lack of maintenance will end up making these roads impassable. In a few seasons, the vegetation will have taken over all it had lost.

A rumbling sound disturbs my tranquility. A vehicle is coming. The clattering motor grows louder. I dash across the road, slosh through the murky water of the ditch, and reach the shadows of the forest.

I hide behind a clump of trees, crouching in the dead leaves. A pickup truck bounces past, its shock absorbers protesting and its exhaust system leaking. The truck passes in front of me, raising a cloud of dust that muddies the border between earth and sky, then rattles along on its way.

Since the blackout, the ground has stopped trembling beneath semis hauling logs, but there is more traffic in the forest. Some people have sought shelter in their cottages and hunting camps. Others have tried to set up shop somewhere new, far from the towns and the main highways. People are wary; they make their calculations, hands on their weapons. Anything can happen at any time. I prefer the depths of the forest to a chance encounter on a logging road.

As evening settles over the underbrush, I come to a pond. The singing of the frogs is deafening. I spot a little building under the black cape of some fir trees. I hide behind a curtain of cattails to keep from being seen. Mosquitoes attack me. Fireflies blink their signal lights. Small creatures slip through the bushes. Nothing else is moving. My lucky day – the cabin is deserted. I go over and climb the slimy wooden steps. Tipped off by the sound of my steps, the frogs go quiet.

The door is locked. I manage to open it from the inside by sticking my arm through the window. The hinges creak. I pull out my flashlight. The cabin is surprisingly tidy. The dishes lined up on the shelves. The bed carefully made. Three empty bottles with candles await their turn on the windowsill. I light all three. A coppery glow spreads across the room. A thin layer of dust shines on every surface. A pair of boots sits at the foot of the bed. Even though it looks like they have been there a long time, I lock the door. Outside, the frogs have struck up their chorus again.

I go through the cupboards and find tea, a jar of peanut butter, canned meat in a sauce, and canned pineapple. I devour everything I can, undress, and sit on the bed, exhausted. My blood is pounding in my swollen knee, my feet stink, and the sores on my collarbones are weeping.

I have too much stuff. I sink into the ground with every step. I look at my bag lying on the floor like a dead horse. I'd like to slice it open and make it lighter. But I've thrown away so much already. My slingshot, my binoculars, and my changes of clothes. Other than my map, compass, tarp, and sleeping bag, all I carry is food and water. They weigh upon me and allow me hope.

I fall back onto the bed. Its soft embrace belongs to the realm of dreams. I lie and watch the candlelight dance until it flickers out in the bottlenecks. Then I fall into a brushy sleep, full of vines, ferns, and dark shapes.

7:15 A.M.

I open my eyes and wonder where I am, surprised not to be surrounded by trees and plants for once. Then I remember and make myself tea on the gas burner. I savour it even if it is insipid, then unfold my map on the table.

The sea and the coastal villages are at the top and to the right, east, near the legend. A few red lines head into the backcountry. Those are the routes leading to the Park. Around them, logging roads are designated by dotted lines. They slip into the hollows of valleys and hairpin their way towards cutting sites. The constellations of black dots denote isolated villages and tall green grass stands for swamps. Otherwise, the rest, all the rest, is forest.

My finger crosses the gradient lines and plateaus, swims across several lakes, conquers the endless mountains and gorges of the Park, then stops at the X written in lead pencil, in the bend of a river. Where my family's hunting camp lies.

To reach it, I figured I'd need two weeks, three at the most. My calculations were way off. I am moving at a snail's pace. I veer off on one detour after another. I can't even imagine when I'll get there. I move forward, every day I move forward, that's all that counts.

As I gather up my things, I notice a watch on the edge of a shelf. An old watch with hands. It is still working. Seven fifteen. I check out the boots by the bed, but they look a couple of sizes too small for me. I pack my bag, slip its weight onto my back, grab my sticks, and go on my way, wearing the watch on my wrist.

I keep up a good pace despite my knee. High above, the leaves reach for the sun. Birds play among the branches. They call back and forth and the sound is deafening. I am always amazed how the silence and immobility of winter have given up their hold on the world.

By afternoon, the air has turned warm and humid. My clothes cling to my skin. The forest is opaque, and I search for water to fill my bottle. At the foot of a slope, the mesh of branches opens up. I figure I have come to a river, then walk onto a cleared area where high-tension pylons stand. With their frail skeletons, they look like glass scarecrows on stilts. They probably link the wind turbines on the coast to the southern part of the country. The cables they hold sketch out heavy undulations against the sky. The forest at their feet has been cut down. Saplings of all shapes have sprung up, but they don't reach the pylons' ankles. For a moment, I enjoy the breeze blowing through this open spot. Normally, you would hear the lines sizzling, the strange and familiar sound of current. Now there is nothing. Just the evening air whistling through the angular bodies of these metallic monsters.

Clouds are piling up over the foothills of the mountains. The drum roll of thunder. I move under the pylons, quickening my pace, and disappear into the forest. It is five thirty. Tonight, I'll need to find shelter. There is bound to be a storm.

An electrical storm.

9:10 P.M.

The wind picks up, the sky clouds over, the night is implacable. I'm walking down a side road bordered by deep ditches. Gusts of wind shake the trees with a backhand blow. Leaves fly past in the timid light of my headlamp. When the first raindrops hit the ground, I scan the skirt of the forest for a place to lay down my tarp.

Lightning cuts the forest into black and white. Through the thicket of shadows, I see the flash of a bright surface. I move faster. The sky is growling. I come upon the angular form of a forestry harvester with its enormous track wheels, long flexible arm, and glasscd-in cabin.

The door is locked. I grab a stone, smash the handle, and climb inside to shelter. Just in time.

I drop my bag and collapse on the seat, relieved to be out of the storm. The rain picks up and hammers the sheet-metal cabin. Lightning splits the sky. In the brief illumination, I can see the instrument panel with its levers, dials, and switches.

For years, endless years, I repaired, patched together, and brought back from the dead any number of cars, tractors, and dump trucks. My whole life revolved around my work as a mechanic. The lightning flashes like memories and the machine that shelters me trembles, as if it wanted to roar back to life.

With my headlamp, I go through the relics scattered across the cabin. Among the waste paper, coffee cups, and plastic packaging, I come across a bag of licorice. The stuff is dried out and leathery. Like chewing on the soles of my boots. I tear off pieces with my teeth and work over each piece endlessly.

I glance in the rear-view mirror. My hair and beard have grown and are slowly covering my clay-coloured face. My eyes are determined but wearing dark circles. I give myself an uneasy grin and watch the crow's feet spread across my face. Everyone in the family has them. I shut off my lamp and listen to the rain pour down on the forest.

The lightning reveals the dark belly of the clouds, the wildly tossing treetops, and the streams of water rushing across the earth. In the stroboscopic light, I am amazed to see several figures trudging, head down, along the muddy road. Their raincoats shine as they flap in the wind. I wipe the condensation off the glass and squint into the darkness, wondering what they are doing there. When the sky lights up again and thunder makes the earth shake, I search again, but the little convoy has disappeared.

The storm rages a while longer, then grows weary and moves on, grumbling. Silence slips from its hiding place and takes over the night again. I turn this way and that, but can't find sleep.

The dashboard has a radio. The idea of hearing the news, music, or even the weather report is tempting. I come back to reality. It is almost eleven at night. I am sitting in the cabin of a machine that hasn't worked for months, its batteries are dead, and, in any case, every radio station in the country has long since stopped broadcasting.

I end up dozing off as the field mice go about their business in the ventilation conduits. In my sleep, I hear them gnawing away at this steel monster from within. They are making their nest there so that one realm will succeed the next.

6:25 A.M.

I get back on the road once first light wipes away the darkness. My feet sink into the marshy path. Among the streams of water, stones, and broken branches, I try to make out some sign of the people who walked past last night. The rain has washed away all trace, though my footprints are fresh and would be visible to anyone. The sign of a man on his own, walking with his eyes on the ground as he leans heavily on his sticks.

A little farther on, the path opens onto a clear-cut zone that still shows the squared-off passages of the machines. Despite the desolation, new growth is springing up everywhere. The brilliant green of the stems and leaves contrasts with the grey rotting stumps and muddy ruts. The air smells of wet earth. I stop and eat a handful of dried fruit. Immediately, a cloud of mosquitoes descends on me. I consult my map, trying in vain to keep them away. A river lies a kilometre ahead. I have no choice; I have to get back onto the road to cross the bridge. A squirrel climbs a notched trunk, stops at my height, stares at my food, then at me. I frighten it off with a quick move of my hand. It disappears into the brush and comes back on my right. It issues a series of strident complaints, telling me I will always be a stranger in these lands.

I slap a mosquito on my cheek, gather my things, and limp off. The day is going to be scorching. Heat haze distorts the horizon. Above the low vegetation left by the loggers, the horizon's mirage is within reach. I don't believe in it for a second.

After several hours walking through an enormous cut zone littered with stumps, I reach the dirt road. I step onto it carefully, then reach an intersection lined with grass and brambles. Signs are nailed on some of the tree trunks. Some have been there for a while, eaten away by time and grown over with moss. Hunting Season, No Entry. Logging Zone C-28. Metal Bridge 4 km. Other signs are newer with brighter colours, addresses, and arrows. Pellerin Family, Party at the Chalet. La Coulée Sector, No Admittance. Angel, We're at Bear Lake.

I head towards the bridge, still vigilant. Tire tracks press into the greasy skin of the road. The little convoy in the storm comes to mind. Maybe they're right, it's better to lie low during the day and travel at night. I reach the top of a slope – there is a car on the shoulder. I step off to the side, ready to disappear into the foliage at the slightest sign of movement. Nothing is moving outside of a few birds chirping among the branches. I move towards the vehicle. My shoulders relax when I spot the flat tires, the thick layer of dust on the metal, and the dry leaves stuck under the windshield wipers. It's a hybrid, a recent model with a numeric screen for a dashboard and electronic controls. No wonder it has stopped running. The driver's side window has been smashed. I look in. Besides a baby seat and some kids' clothes in the back, there are only empty containers, cloth bags, and old newspapers. I lean inside. I want to read the headlines. "Government Divided." "More Interruptions Expected." "Army Mobilized to Help Population." Something is buzzing close by and I jump. My skin is on fire. I cry out, crush the insect, and back off. A swarm of wasps lives in the car. Some of them attack. I take off, waving my arms uselessly in the air.

I stop farther on, much farther on, a little stunned and out of breath. I throw down my pack and pull off my shirt. The stings are swollen and painful. Three on my arm, one on the back of my neck, the rest scattered across my torso. I pour water over them, hoping to calm the sting, but that does no good. I sit down on my pack and let the pain move through me, knowing it will fade sooner or later.

Twenty minutes later, I'm on my way again, along the road that splits the opaque mass of trees. Up ahead, under a clear blue metallic sky, I see the skeletal form of the iron bridge.

It stretches between the two banks, supported by a crisscross of steel beams. Rust has attacked the structure. In the sunlight, its reddish hue stands out against the black spruce. I come closer and see the big tree trunk blocking access. I crouch down behind some bushes. It's a roadblock, maybe. I wait and listen to the powerful current of the river. The day is going by, my legs are turning numb, everything seems quiet. I take my chance.

Just as I decide to move, a pickup comes up behind me. I scarcely have time to hide in the thicket again. I have my pack in my arms and I'm holding my breath. They must have seen me. But the truck passes and heads for the bridge. Then it slows and stops in front of the log roadblock. I look up. Three guys climb down from the back. One of them goes over to the driver and they have a short conversation. The driver points to the obstacle. The others take a look around. The driver swears and pounds the steering wheel. The three guys climb back into the truck. They turn around and speed off the way they came. The pistons knock furiously in the cylinders. The sound fades, grows weaker, and is swallowed up by the curtain of the forest.

I venture out of my hiding place, cross onto the bridge, and step over the impressive log. It is solidly attached to the bridge deck by chains and padlocks. I make sure it's not a booby trap, then move past it. Below, the muddy water boils. Upstream, the banks have collapsed into the riverbed and uprooted trees slant down from their former heights. Downstream, everything rushes towards the sea. The raging current is so loud someone could call my name and I wouldn't hear.

I reach the other side, reassured by the solid ground under my feet. I move away from the roaring river and leave the dirt road. It is a relief to recover the familiar murmur of the underbrush.

2:45 P.M.

For hours, I've been walking to the metallic sound of my empty water bottle hanging from my pack. The afternoon air is sticky. My mouth is pasty and I'm thirsty. So thirsty I can't think of anything else. I should have filled my bottle yesterday at the river. I am crossing through an endless pine wood, and with each step, the carpet of reddish dry needles whispers underfoot. The only water in sight is the sweat running down my face.

Slowly, the forest changes its look. A few rocks are visible at certain points. The pines give way to deciduous trees, the smell of sun-heated resin fades, and soon I come upon a little spring making its way between the joined hands of the roots. I slake my thirst with the trickle of cold water. I feel my body relaxing. Life returns. I fill my bottle, test my knee, and get moving again.

The afternoon light is playful, the forest opens up before me, I'm making good time. But I stop when I hear voices ahead, muffled by the distance. I move forward carefully, ready to hide if I need to, then stumble upon a heap of gravel grown over with wild wheat. The voices grow louder, blending in with the nasal complaint of the crows overhead. I hesitate, but curiosity gets the better of me. I drop my pack behind a rock and climb up the slope, using the bushes to steady me. At the top, there is an empty plot of land. In the middle is an enormous hole filled with garbage, junk, and scrap metal. A dump. It's not on my map. There must be many others like it. Since they have stopped burning their garbage, cities have been shipping their trash into the forest, to dumps no one can see.

A dozen men and women are working the site, surrounded by plastic bags, disassembled furniture, and garbage of every type. I slip between wrecked cars and a row of appliances to observe the scene without being spotted. The people are digging through the heap, ripping open bags, setting aside all kinds of objects. Clouds of crows caw and treat themselves to what the humans have offered them. Most of the diggers are wearing handkerchiefs over their mouths and noses. I hear them talking, but can't make out what they are saying. From time to time, a burst of laughter in the air. They are throwing their treasures into a trailer attached to a van and the back of a pickup. Mattresses and furniture have been tied to the roofs. Leaning on one of the vehicles, a guy with a rifle and a cigarette in his mouth is watching the edge of the woods. Probably keeping an eye out for bears.

The dump is a world of its own. Even if no truck has come to deliver a load here since the power went out, the place is alive with flies, vermin, and scavengers.

I notice two other people off to the side, digging through the pit. A man and a child. I watch them pile their treasures into a supermarket cart. They gauge their little heap of objects, as if making a decision, then get on the road heading south, pushing their cart through the dust. Their progress is resigned. But at least there are two of them.

I back off, but trip over an old piece of scrap metal that clatters. The silence that follows is frightening. I turn around and a bullet whizzes past me, ricocheting farther on. My heart pounds. The explosion echoes in the pit. I hit the ground, then move down the slope on all fours, grab my pack, and scurry off like a scared animal. I stop to catch my breath and check to see if the bullet hit me. My knee cartilage sends up pain signals. The blisters on my feet popped when I ran. Shaken, I stretch out on the ground, on the rich humus.

Since the power went out, everything has changed, but the laws of the forest remain. Either you step forward and defend your territory, or humble yourself and go your way, your back bent.

8:05 P.M.

I'm following a four-by-four track on the edge of a fallow field. The spruce push their heads timidly through the jungle of greedy young deciduous trees. They are sombre, planted in endless rows by reforestation teams.

At the end of the day, I come face to face with a fawn, still showing its white markings. A few leaps and it is gone. I spot a hunting blind set up on a metal scaffold. I slip behind the foliage and wait to see if the business end of a rifle will come gunning for me again. Nothing of the sort. I step out of my hiding place and move forward carefully. The blind has been deserted. I climb the ladder. The little shelter is in a miserable state, but the roof's membrane has held up. On the windowsill is an ashtray full of butts, a book of crossword puzzles swollen with humidity, and a box of granola bars. Excellent. I drop my pack, push the folding chair to one side, and with a piece of cardboard sweep the dead flies off the floor. I sit down and lean against the plywood wall. I try to open the puzzle book, but mould has glued the pages together. I choose the most promising cigarette butt and smoke it, listening to the whisper of falling twilight. The smoke whirls through my lungs and rolls out of my mouth in long plumes. Its tarry essence makes me sick, but it's good all the same. I let vertigo take me in its arms and dance me in circles.

Howling echoes in the distance. Darkness freezes as the sound approaches. Wolves. They must be tracking the fawn.

In the tall grass around the blind, I hear twigs snapping. Then a high-pitched lament tears through the peace of this place. Guttural sounds, jaws ripping through flesh, hungry growls.

I lie down in these narrow confines and smoke a second cigarette butt. The eternal dance of predators and prey. The endless war of chance and necessity. The survival of the fittest, safety in numbers, the cover of darkness.

7:30 A.M.

There is no path through this sector. Three days of orienting with my compass. The forest is dense and voracious. In their savage competition for sunlight, trees and plants take all the space they can. My progress is slow, but I keep moving forward, every day closer to my goal. I sleep where I can and take off again at first light. I cut my way through the green wall of flora, the dusty roads, the yellow eyes of beasts. I have a good supply of food in my bag and my hands can still grasp my walking sticks. Everything ahead of me awaits, irremediable. Everything behind me has stopped existing.

Soon, already, again, shadows proliferate beneath the canopy, and despite my will, my knee is beginning to weaken. I come upon a narrow clearing. An opening in the endless ceiling of leaves. This is where I will spend the night.

I nibble on some crackers with peanut butter, then change the bandages on my shoulders. I would love to make a fire, but I don't want to risk attracting attention. I hang my pack from a branch, unroll my tarp, and get into my sleeping bag. An owl hoots among the trees. Above, the starry slate of the sky contrasts with the forest's robe.

Mosquitoes buzz in my ear. I chase them off, turn once, then again, feeling the knots of the roots beneath my aching body. I am exhausted, but sleep does not oblige. My hands behind my head, I question the nebulous stars in the sky.

The faces of the men and women I have met since the power went off haunt me. I wonder where they are now.

Hard to say – the world from before has been buried with its interrupted destinies and promises. The world after is uncertainty, and it's better not to listen to that. Between the two, everyone is doing what they can to give meaning to their lives.

A rustling in the dead leaves puts me on high alert. I lift my head and am blinded by the night. Twigs crack. I tell myself it's only a shrew or a raccoon, but the fear of wolves won't leave me alone. The darkness that reigns beneath the trees absorbs everything as I listen to the reassuring ticking of my watch. I fall back onto the tarp and hope deep sleep will come, knowing very well that the forest never rests.

4:10 P.M.

I take a break by the edge of a stream. I watch the water flow past, jealous of its quickness, its fluidity, the easy way it moves forward. I wiggle my toes deep in my dank boots. I am a runt, hunted down. I take deep breaths, splash fresh water on my face, but every day fatigue wraps tighter around me.

I eat one of the granola bars I found a while back and study a wild vine climbing up a tree, taking it over little by little, slowly suffocating it. More than the claws of beasts or the sights of firearms or the mesh of the forest, weariness is the black queen of this place.

I take a deep breath and start walking. The air smells of plants. Exposed roots snake across the sinuous path. Here and there, I pass boulders that are like pebbles left by a stumbling giant ages ago to help find the way back. On one of them, through the little trees and green moss that is almost blue, I spot a pheasant. I lean on my sticks to watch it. It looks back at me. It wonders about me, waits, then loses interest, turns its head, and starts pecking at the ground nonchalantly. A shiver runs through me. The effect of hunger. Nuts, canned goods, and granola bars aren't enough. My heart is racing. I need meat. The pheasant seems to sense my thoughts. It sizes me up one last time, then ambles off.

I remember the small game we used to prepare at our hunting camp when I was a kid. I remember the acrid scent of the viscera, the viscous mass of offal, the fur and feathers in the dirt, the tall cedars all around, the way my uncles looked, my aunts laughed, the tasty flesh of our meals, the noisy card games, the dried blood beneath our nails.

I wriggle out from under my pack, lean over for a stone, and circle the rock. I spot the bird not far away. I move closer, gripping the stone in my hand. The bird pays me no mind. I concentrate, then let fly with my shot. My bullet whistles through the air, then flies into the labyrinth of dead leaves, just above my target. The pheasant lifts its neck nervously, is still for a moment, then goes back to pecking at the ground. I pick up another stone and try my luck again. This time I think I've hit it, but after some small agitation, it flies off to shelter on a tree branch.

Shit.

I stand there at a loss. Suddenly the pheasant falls from its branch and hits the ground, flapping its wings heavily. I rejoice. I got it!

But the bird isn't dead. It picks itself up and disappears into the bushes. I run my tongue over my canines and take off after the bird, rushing through the brush and over dead trunks. Without the weight of my pack, my legs lift me and defy gravity. Fatigue is a thing of the past as I sprint by the low branches as if nothing else existed in this dense forest but a wounded pheasant that has awakened my meat-eater's instincts.

I stop. I've spotted my prey. Just a shadow between two stumps. I look around. White birches shoot skyward like arrows over a sea of ferns. My blood pounds for no reason now. Dead or alive, the pheasant could be anywhere. I scan the forest feverishly. After a while, I don't know where to look anymore, my shoulders droop, and I lose hope. The hunter returns empty-handed.

I retrace my steps painfully. No other choice but more peanut butter. I trip and catch myself just in time, bracing myself against a tree. The bark crumbles like paper beneath my hand. I look up. The forest is an endless bower. It looks the same on all sides. The sun is still high in the sky. The trees bow in its direction as I go zigzagging in search of a clue to where the path is, the big rock, my walking sticks pushed into the ground, the colours of my backpack. Nothing. I go from one clearing to the next, urged on by false hope. Emptiness grips my heart. My pack. Without it, I'm just a vulnerable animal far from its destination.

I come to the bottom of a slope. My stomach is grumbling. My knee pains me with every step. My head weighs a ton. In front of me stands a dead tree in the crushing greenness of the forest. Its fleshless arms reach for the sky. A ghost imploring the heavens.

It is a quarter to five. I try and get a hold of myself. I'm going to find the path, recover my pack, eat something, and continue on my way. Soon, I will cross through the Park to my family's camp. My aunts and uncles will be surprised to see me, but they'll welcome me as if they had been waiting all along.

Above, the trees hold hands and form a wide, diaphanous dome. The light is filtered by the stained glass of leaves and branches. I move through this temple made of living pillars and hear them whispering vague messages. I push aside a broken branch in my way, but go about it wrong, and it snaps back in my face like a whip. Blood flows from my nose. I tip back my head until it slows, then stops completely. I go back to walking with the taste of iron in my mouth.

As I move along the slope, I push aside ferns, hoping to find my own trail. Outside of tracks made by animals, there is nothing to help me. I go on, seeing my pack in every spot in the forest. I should have done like the stumbling giant and left rocks along the way. Maybe I could climb a tree and reconnoitre from above. But from that perspective I would see no more than a patchwork of leaves and needles fighting for a share of the light.

I try to get oriented and find landmarks, but there is nothing but the savage, bitter fabric of trees, living and dead. My solitude is complete. I try and work up the courage, but I don't have the strength to hold back my despair. In the middle of the journey of my life, and I am lost in a forest dark.

Something is moving. I squint and spot two furry arrows rolling one on top of the other down a mound of earth. They spring to their feet, scratch at each other, then face me. Their tawny coats are spotted with black, their short tails and the elegant triangles of their ears leave no doubt. Two young lynx. Their mother can't be far. As soon as the two wildcats go back to their play, I retreat, break into a run, flee. One more time.

This time I don't stop, afraid of the claws sinking into my back. I'm lost and limping. The ideal prey for a feline to bring back to her young to teach them how to kill. I bull my way through bushes, my eyes closed. I hardly know what I'm doing. The mosquitoes harass me. They buzz in my ears and get into my mouth and nose. I whirl around on myself, waving my arms, enraged, out of control. The path is nowhere. My watch is useless. I turn circles like its two hands. My knee gives way, I stumble in the tall grass. I go to shout, but no noise comes out of my mouth. I rage against my fate. When I get to my feet again, my vision is dotted with black spots. I blink them away, leaning against a stump; I can hardly see anything that stands before me. My body is bathed in sweat. My arms and legs are numb. The air in my lungs is heavy. I lift my hand towards the sky as if someone were there to grasp it.

Then the forest wavers and falls.

7:00 P.M.

I open my eyes halfway. I am lying on the ground in the middle of the grass and twigs. I shift and check my watch. More than two hours stretched out like this, without moving. The evening has turned the sky metallic blue. I feel a little nauseous, but at least my dizziness has gone. I get painfully to my knees and consider my surroundings. I feel like I'm being watched, and fear the presence of wolves behind the branches. I'm on my guard as I gather my wits. It's late, I have no idea where I am, no more than I know where I should go next. My map, my compass, my flashlight – everything is in my pack. I breathe in hard, swear, and pound the ground. I look up towards the crown of trees. They have separated from the sky and are leaning over me like curious animals.

I lift myself to my feet and take a few steps.

How come you're limping?

I freeze. I might as well have been struck by lightning.

How come you're limping?

I hear my blood rattling through my body. I'm hungry, I'm thirsty, I'm exhausted. My brain must be playing tricks on me. I turn slowly on the axis of my being. Behind, in the lace of ferns, is a figure. A boy. Twelve years old or so. He is watching me, his head to one side. His skin is tanned, his blond hair uncombed, his eyes are as black as coal. He is wearing a bag over his shoulder, and in one hand, he is holding a dead pheasant.

7:05 P.M.

How come you're limping?

I stare at the boy in astonishment. He steps forward and sits down on a rock cross-legged. His eyes are bright and lively, a far cry from his dirty clothes.

It was wounded, he tells me, swinging the pheasant by its feet. It let me come near, it looked at me like this, sideways. I stretched out my hand and wrung its neck.

I shake my head, left to right, and try and get a hold of myself. I'm lost in the middle of the forest, my throat is dry, and my hands are trembling, and here's a little kid who doesn't seem to be lost, or dead tired, or starving to death, or dying of thirst, or scared. As if he had fallen out of the sky.

He doesn't understand why I can't speak. He pushes the pheasant into his bag.

What are you doing here? I stammer. Where are your parents?

The boy gazes at me, impassive. I scan the underbrush. With the dew, the ferns look phosphorescent. Twilight is falling. Soon, darkness.

There's a path around here somewhere. Do you know where?

The boy smiles, amused, but doesn't answer or move. He is waiting.

A car crash, I tell him, pointing at my knee. That's why I limp.

The memory of the pain, the fever, my legs incarcerated in splints torment me a moment.

What kind of crash?

Two eyes shining in the middle of the road. Swerving. Impact. Losing control.

What kind of animal? Did it die? he pushes on, since I am lost in my thoughts.

Yes. On the spot.

He thinks about that for a moment, then rises to his feet.

Come on, follow me. The path isn't far.

The shadows of evening draw back a little. My young guide walks fast and I work to keep up. We move through branches and up a steep slope. The ground is unstable. I have to grab hold of roots and small trees to keep from falling.

Let's go, he calls, hands on his hips, this way.

It's completely dark by the time our feet reach the path. The forest is a shadowy, noisy presence. We move forward blindly. Farther on, by a large shapeless rock, we stumble over my pack. My relief is immediate. I am saved. I bend down, take my bottle, and swallow great mouthfuls of water.

Thanks, I tell him, collapsing next to my pack. What's your name?

The boy turns on his heels and fades into the darkness.

Don't go!

I wonder if the boy wasn't the fruit of my imagination. Fine, I recovered my backpack, but I might be losing my mind. Then I hear sounds in the forest. My new companion is coming back with bark, twigs, and bits of wood. He kneels down to build a fire.

No, I tell him, don't do that.

He looks at me, not understanding.

We might get found out.

So? he replies, striking a match.

At first I'm tense, but I relax as the light of the flames

shines upon us and lights our dirty faces, cutting a piece out of the night. I stretch out my hands, hypnotized by the burning, crackling wood. Its heat embraces me, rocks me, envelops me.

The boy takes the pheasant from his bag, puts his feet on its wings, and pulls on its legs to separate the breast. He quickly runs two sticks through the pieces of meat and holds them over the fire. I watch, fascinated, but piqued as well by his mysterious presence. A few embers climb into the air. I clear my throat.

Tell me, don't you think your parents will be worried? Won't they come looking for you?

No risk of that, he tells me, then changes the conversation. That's a pretty big bag you're carrying. It must be heavy.

Tomorrow I'll help you find them. Do you live around here?

The boy shrugs his shoulders, checks on the meat, then hands me my share. I put off my questions. I thank him and bite into the flesh. My mouth waters.

What time is it? he asks, pointing at my watch with his chin.

The question strikes me as strange. I look at my wrist. The figures on the dial are suddenly meaningless next to the firelight, the height of the trees, the depth of the night.

Five after ten, I tell him.

He bursts out laughing, chewing noisily. The meal over, he wipes his hands on the grass and throws more wood on the fire. The flames leap higher, showing us the ribs of the vault above our heads.

I use the sudden light to check my itinerary. When he sees me unfolding the map, my new friend's eyes light up as if we were going in search of Treasure Island. He comes and stands next to me and leans over the map. He points to the coastal villages at the top, by the legend. He speaks their names, drawing back better to situate them in the immensity of space, then examines the sinuous design of the topography that occupies the middle of the land.

What are all those lines?

Contour lines. They show the elevation. The closer together they are, the rougher the terrain. The farther apart, the flatter the land.

He evaluates the mountains and valleys and rivers. Then puts his finger on the X written in pencil.

What's that?

My family's camp.

That's where you're going?

I nod. He is pensive. I ask him about his parents again. His face shuts down, but I push on.

Tell me, what are you doing here? Are you lost?

He pretends not to understand. He walks away, picks up a pheasant feather from the ground, runs the sharp end of it over his lips a few times, then throws it into the fire. I give up, bent by fatigue, heavy with the effort of digestion. I unroll my tarp and sleeping bag. The boy makes a heap of pine branches and lies down, his head on his small pack, wrapped in a narrow survival blanket, gold on one side, silver on the other. It looks like a cape.

The fire slowly burns down and the flames lie low in the embers. In the reddish glow, the boy and I look at each other.

Olio, he says before turning over. My name is Olio.

Okay, I say, satisfied. Good night, Olio.

Good night.

5:40 A.M.

I wake up with first light. Olio is gone, along with his bag. I search for him in the morning mist, but it's no use. Nothing left but his little pallet of branches. I am relieved at the thought that he has returned home to his family. I eat a handful of nuts and pack up my things, a routine by now.

You ready? a voice above me calls.

I look up. Standing on the big rock covered with moss and low bushes is the boy, his bag slung over his shoulder.

I agree without really thinking – ready for what? Olio stretches out his arms and jumps, lands at my side like a cat, and bounces down the path. I take up my pack and my sticks and follow him, leaving solitude behind.

Olio walks fast. I take long strides, but he barely touches the ground. From time to time, he waits for me at a turn in the path. Sometimes I spot him in the distance, turning over stones. I'd like to know what he's after, but he starts moving as soon as I come near.

In the afternoon, we come to wetlands. Vegetation has swallowed the path and we advance blindly through a sea of brush. I am having more and more trouble.

Just do like me, Olio says, watching me struggle. First your head, then your body. Easy. All animals do that.

I push forward, fighting the weir of branches. Despite my efforts, they grab me, hold me back, lacerate me. My pack slows me down, my boots are heavy with clay. It's a battle until the forest thins out.

That's it, I agree, panting. First your head, then your body.

That evening, we set up camp in a grove of larches. I am wiped out. But comforted by the distance we covered today. Strangely, my knee isn't causing too much pain.

Olio takes a worm from a small jar. That's what he was looking for under the stones.

Look, he says, cutting it in two with his thumb and index finger. He's not dead. First he was alone, now he's two.

He laughs at my incredulity, takes a spool of fishing line and a few hooks from his bag, then disappears into the trees.

I kick off my wet boots and dry my smelly clothes on a branch. I don't like the look of the strips of dead skin and hardened spurs on my feet. Lesions run along my collarbones from carrying my pack. The light is slowly fading. The soft green of larch needles stands out against the violet sky. I breathe in deeply, rub my knee, and surrender to the forest. The distant murmur of a stream joins the chirping of insects. The breeze whistles in the treetops. Fledglings call out for food from a nearby nest.

I pour the contents of my pack on the ground and take inventory of my supplies. Canned fruit, sardines, four packets of powdered soup, a chocolate bar, and a little dried fruit and nuts. Not much. Especially for two people.

Olio comes back just before nightfall with a dozen small trout strung up by the gills, hanging from a branch. We light a fire and cook the fish on a hot stone. Their flesh is pink and delicate. An absolute feast. After we finish, Olio turns to me.

In the city, what do you think people are eating?

I'm not sure, I admit, but there are big warehouses, supermarkets, containers. And with the power not coming back, people are organizing. Who knows, by now maybe they have gardens on every roof!

Olio looks at me wide-eyed. I ask him again if he comes from the city.

Yes and no, he tells me, cleaning his teeth with a twig. I lived in the suburbs.

I think of the cars abandoned on urban expressways, the boarded-up windows of apartment towers, the panicked population picking over looted stores.

A while after the blackout, Olio continues, we packed our stuff in the car and left. My parents, my brother, and me. There were traffic jams everywhere. My mother and father took turns at the wheel until we got to the cabin. We spent the summer there. At first it was like vacation. Fishing, campfires, the woods.

The sound of a cracking branch echoes in the cavern of the night. I jump. The boy gives me a mocking look.

We've been spotted, quick, run, he jokes.

I frown, irritated, and retreat into my sleeping bag. The embers slip into their nest of ash and the ligneous darkness takes over. I am on the edge of the world of dreams when Olio brings me back.

Where do you come from?

A little mining village. Two weeks' walk from here.

Why are you going to your family's camp?

My aunts and uncles have been there since last fall.

Why didn't you go with them?

I was hurt. I point to my knee. I couldn't even stand up.

They left without you.

They didn't have the choice.

Oh, he says, surprised. You think they'll be happy to see you?

They'll be surprised, for sure. I haven't set foot in that camp for over ten years.

What's it like there?

There are no roads in the sector. Normally we leave the

vehicles at the dock and canoe the rest of the way in. The river is green and quiet. It flows strongly and there are deep spots. The camp is set back in a bend, under cedar trees that are a hundred years old.

Olio lies down near me, arms behind his head.

You'll see, the camp isn't very big, but there's always room.

We listen to the sounds of the night and say no more. Olio has fallen asleep, or at least I think so. I lift my head towards the constellations and feel the great black hole inside me shrinking. Memories step forward and pay no heed to my fatigue. When I was this boy's age, there were always parties in my family. The table overflowing with food, the conversations running together, a pile of coats in the guest room. My cousin Sylvia and I would hide for hours inside this mountain of perfume. When everyone burst out laughing in the next room, the walls would tremble, the horde of happy ogres shook them, the starving, implacable ogres of my family.

Olio turns to me. His eyes are open.

Pigeons and rats, he says. In the city, after all this time, that's what people are eating.

3:15 P.M.

Olio and I have been walking together for several days now. I don't understand the tacit agreement that binds us. Our bodies move through the humidity and heat of the forest. Our eyes have grown accustomed to the green shadows. With every step, we learn to know each other.

What did you do before? he asks as we travel down a long tunnel of trees, tortuous, turning upon themselves, their limbs embracing.

I was a mechanic in a refinery.

Do you miss your job?

A great emptiness swallows me from inside. I stop and look at my hands. Instead of being black with grease, they are covered in lines of earth. My life before is a distant memory. A withered plant. I remember the smell of exhaust systems, the racket of pneumatic tools, equipment boxes, garage doors. Otherwise, everything else is contained in a few furtive moments, untrustworthy impressions, yellowed pictures. The power failure changed the course of our lives, it pushed our eyes out of perspective, it dismantled our hopes.

I sure don't miss school, Olio tells me, hanging onto a branch above us.

He swings from it, feet in the air, then drops to the ground and slips between the trees. I take up my sticks and follow in his wake. A little farther on, the forest is split in two by a long metal conduit set above the ground on small stilts.

What's that?
A pipeline. It probably goes to the refineries in the South.
That's where you worked?
No. I was in the West. The other side of the continent.
Why so far?
Because of my father, I say, ending the conversation.

I move down the grassy corridor along the pipeline. Olio passes me and climbs onto the enormous construction. He performs a balancing act in perfect equilibrium. Not far, deer graze with no thought for us.

What did your father do? he asks.
He was a mechanic.
Olio watches me a moment.
Listen, he tells me, tapping his foot against the metal. It's hollow.

A gunshot echoes across the clearing. We duck. It's a reflex. The deer dash off. One of them is wounded and soon collapses. We hear shouting. Hunters are running in our direction. Olio jumps off the pipeline and moves towards the scene, drawn to it. I urge him to come back. He refuses. I shoot out my hand, grab his arm, and pull him back. He struggles. My grip is too strong for him. When we are well hidden in the protective net of the branches, I kneel down and look him in the eye.

I don't know how things are where you're from, but here, the forest is full of people. And believe me, you're better off not meeting any of them.

Olio stares back at me.

And when I tell you to come with me, I warn him, you come with me.

Olio looks away. End of lecture. I move off without looking back. A half-hour later, I'm relieved when I hear his footsteps behind me.

We enter a sector where spruce has been planted. The

close-set line of trunks reaches up like arrows. We go past these endless corridors, keeping our distance. Two taciturn beings on the cross-ruled territory of an artificial forest. We take a break and share a can of sardines.

That evening, we stop on a mountaintop whose steep slopes have been spared by the forestry industry. We set up camp between two rocky outcrops. The light of day's end lengthens the shadows of the small trees that have taken root in the cracks. Olio inspects the surroundings, waving a stick in the air as if fencing with the horizon.

Come and look! he calls.

I get to my feet to go see. On the rocky wall in front of him is an engraving scratched into the lichen. The drawing is clear enough despite the erosion caused by weather. A winged wolf ridden by two tiny human shapes.

Who would have done that? Olio asks.

The people who lived here a long time ago.

Really?

Before the pipelines and the forestry harvesters.

He runs his hands over the lines drawn into the rock. I watch him and think of the fragile intersection of the centuries. By the time we return to our camp, the sun has dived below the horizon. Edged by an orange sky, the mountains fade into one another, forming a long crenellated wall.

Over there, that's the Park.

Olio doesn't understand.

Before the power went out, people would go hiking there in the summer and skiing at the Station in winter.

And on the other side, that's the sea, right?

No. The other side is my family's camp. The sea is farther on.

The breeze picks up. We hear it blowing through the stunted pines. Olio questions the landscape.

Imagine if we could fly! he says.

We'd need a place to land.

With a float plane, you can land on any kind of water, he replies, an answer for everything, so why not the sea? I hear there are wind-power farms along the coast. Do you think they're still working?

Darkness settles, filling the gullies, flattening the landscape. In the silence of the evening, thin columns of smoke rise above the tree canopy. Many of us have turned to the forest. I wonder what life in the coastal villages is like. I look to my young friend.

Yes, I think they're still working. When the wind blows.

A vehicle's headlights draw a long curving line across the dark valley.

It's like a falling star, Olio says.

Make a wish, I tease him.

He closes his eyes, concentrates, then opens them again. Well?

I did, he says with startling sincerity.

A few minutes later, he is asleep under his golden cape, close by, with a grin on his face. I feel the warmth of his breath. I lift my head to the sky that curls slowly around the North Star and think of the ancient wolf with his wings and tiny passengers.

1:50 P.M.

We climb up a narrow ravine and reach a spot where a clump of short grass is growing, reddened by the sun. We sit down side by side and drink some water and gaze at two trees wrapped around each other. It is hard to say if they are supporting each other or holding each other back. Skillfully, Olio catches a fly that was buzzing around him. He watches it struggle in his hand, then he pulls off its wings and legs, sets it on a rock, and observes it carefully.

I take out the map. As the crow flies, it looks like we're close to the Park. But we have another dozen days of walking ahead of us, because there is a lake to get around. I'm still limping a little, though my knee is getting better. And the sores on my collarbones have almost healed. No wonder – my pack is getting lighter by the day. We have managed to catch a pheasant and some trout, but soon we will have eaten through my supplies. If we want to reach my family's camp before the summer heat, we will need dried food, things that keep. We can't spend all our time fishing and chasing after small game.

According to the map, we will soon come to a dirt road. Then a small village a few kilometres farther on. A handful of houses and an old sawmill, probably the only chance to get supplies for a while. But it's a detour and people must be living there. I'd rather avoid the place, but we'll have to take a chance.

I chew on a stalk of grass and watch ants carrying the

wingless fly towards their hideout. They will devour it later. I lift my head. Olio is stretched out in the grass, stuffing his face with strawberries.

What's the problem? he teases me. You're afraid the sawmill people will take us prisoner and lock us up until they decide to eat us?

He laughs at his own joke, which strikes me as crude. I look away, fold up the map, and start walking again, tapping my sticks against the rock. He catches up to me, his mouth and fingers stained bright red.

Tell me, he begins, where were you when the lights went out?

At work. I was fixing a truck. When I went outside to see what was going on, it was raining. And you?

In school. In the afternoon. It was a nice day. Plenty of light coming in the windows. No one even knew until class was over. The bell didn't ring.

We reach the edge of the logging road. I motion to Olio to stop. His big black eyes are defiant. I lean over and put my finger to my lips and listen. I hear a vehicle coming, but it is only the wind in the pines. I step out of the woods and wave to Olio to follow. The sun reflects off the road hemmed in between the hermetic walls of vegetation. The scratching of cicadas rises from the thickets.

We come to a crossroads with a bouquet of signs. Here, too, some of them date from before the blackout. Sawmill Crossing, 30 km/h Max. Beaver Lake, 6 km. Danger, Truck Crossing. Some stand out with their big letters written in spray paint on lengths of plywood. Olio reads them out loud; it's a game.

Round-lake-sector, private, at-your-own-risk. Access-to-relay-road, toll-charged. crotchety-lake-township, follow-blue-ribbons. Trout-lake, proof-of-residence-required.

We head towards the sawmill, but a few steps later, the

sound of an engine catches us off guard. We glance at each other. A motor turning and going nowhere. The revving rises and falls, then stops altogether. The silence is heavy with doubt as if we were the only ones left in the world. Ahead, the road curves and bushes cut off our view.

Let's go through the woods, I tell Olio, putting my hand on his shoulder. Come on.

He pushes my arm away and heads down the road. I try and catch him. The motor roars again, and I hear men shouting.

Wait, get back here!

Olio keeps going, ignoring me completely. I curse and hurry after him. Through the bushes, I spot the metallic reflection of a car body. A Jeep bogged down on the sandy shoulder. Two guys turning circles like impatient animals. They're talking, more like arguing. They don't seem to have noticed us. I crouch down at the edge of the road, clench my jaw, and hiss at the boy.

Hide, they're going to see you.

Olio moves easily towards the Jeep as the enamel on my teeth shatters under the pressure. I look away. When the two men go quiet, I know they have spotted him standing in the middle of the road with his dirty hair, his bag slung across his body, and his indolent look.

I swear and pound the earth with the palm of my hand. I take a breath, stand up, and show myself, too. The guys spring into action when they see me appear after Olio. One of them thrusts out his chest, hands on his hips. The other rushes back to the Jeep and hides behind the door. Olio turns and gives me a sarcastic look.

The first guy has a moustache and his hair is combed to one side. The second is skinny and wearing a lumberjack shirt too big for him. There are skid marks on the gravel and the Jeep looks completely stuck at the edge of the road.

What do you want? Where are you coming from? the skinny one wants to know.

You going to the sawmill? the moustache asks.

Olio moves forward and stops right next to them. He considers their situation a moment.

Are you guys stuck? he asks.

Yes, the moustache answers hesitantly, embarrassed. We skidded off.

He raises his head to me and mimes the accident with his arms.

You skidded off, the skinny one corrects him as he stands up, rifle at the ready. You skidded off the road because you took the turn too fast.

You can talk, you never drive, the moustache retorts.

The men glare at each other.

My uncle and I are going to Snake Lake, Olio says. His self-assurance is disconcerting.

Don't know it, the moustache mutters, wiping his forehead. We're going to the Station. But now, the harder we try to get out of this trap, the more we sink in.

We can help, Olio offers, looking back at me.

I nod, though I don't much care for the boy's attitude. I circle the Jeep to get an idea of the situation. The skinny guy follows me. I tell them that if all three of us push, we should be able to do it. I set Olio at the wheel, start the motor, and tell him to wait for my signal. On the back seat and in the trunk, boxes and bags are piled. Olio's eyes glitter. I repeat my instructions and take up position on the side with the two guys. We push all we can, but as soon as Olio hits the gas pedal, the back wheels spin uselessly and shoot stones at our legs. The Jeep sinks deeper into the sandy shoulder. We cease operations.

We're too heavy, the moustache decides. He is puffing with discouragement. We'll have to unload.

His friend is boiling mad. It's ridiculous. All that because of a wrong move. The two pals raise their voices. I go up and have a look at the Jeep's instruments.

Push down on that lever, I tell the boy. Push down the lever and hit the gas, but very, very slowly.

Get out of the way! I warn the men.

Olio gives it a little gas and the Jeep pulls itself out of the shoulder without us even having to push. The two guys stand there in disbelief. Olio stops the vehicle a little farther on.

Four-wheel drive is there for a reason, I tell the men.

I told you so, the skinny one grumbles.

The moustache turns red and scratches his head. Then he notices the terrible state of our clothes and offers to drive us somewhere.

His friend elbows him. It's risky, he whispers, and anyway, they don't have room. And people say there's a checkpoint at the sawmill. They don't want to attract attention. He glances at his watch and announces that it's already three thirty.

I look at my watch, too, a few seconds later. The two guys argue. I think about the moustache's offer. If they really are going to the Station, that would be quite the shortcut. I look towards Olio. He is walking around the Jeep, slamming the doors.

We can always make room for them if we put stuff on the roof, the moustache says.

What's that kid doing? the skinny one asks nervously, pointing at Olio.

Playing, I tell him casually.

The two pals go on arguing. The skinny one is about to give in when Olio comes back and interrupts them.

I told you, we're going to Snake Lake. That's not in the same direction.

I don't get it, but I'm relieved.

Okay, then, let's get on the road! the skinny guy resolves, heading for the Jeep.

The moustache thanks us. He digs around in his pockets and takes out a pack of salted almonds and gives it to Olio.

Good luck, he stammers, turning towards the vehicle, and happy travels.

A few seconds later, the Jeep takes off down the gravel road. We watch them fade into the landscape, and the song of the insects is master again.

Here, Olio orders, pulling me by the sleeve, come and see.

In the grass growing in the ditch, near where the Jeep stopped, I see potatoes, a sack of oats, canned fruit, and some packets of dried food.

We're a great team, he smiles, don't you think?

I can't help but smile. We pick up the loot and fill our packs. My load is heavier again, but the weight is reassuring. Before heading out again, I turn to Olio.

Where is this Snake Lake of yours?

Here, he tells me, pointing to the exact spot between his nose and his two eyes. Right here.

11:30 A.M.

The good weather has held since we got back in the forest with our new supplies. Above our heads, the trees are a tapestry over the sky, drinking up the light. At our feet, the ground is covered with wide, dark-leafed plants that enjoy the little sun they can find. We move through this two-tiered world until we reach a river. My map tells me there is no road or bridge in the area. We follow the bank for a while, then find a place to ford the river.

I put my hand in the water. The contrast with the air is striking. Olio takes off his clothes, ties them onto his bag, and ventures into the water. It comes up to his chest. He is holding his bag in his arms, and instead of fighting the current, he takes long steps through it towards the other shore. For a second I am afraid he will be swept away, but he does very well. A little like he was weightless.

I undress and try my luck, a walking stick in one hand and my pack like a bundle of firewood on my shoulder. The sun bounces blinding flashes of light off the river and it isn't easy to see where I should put my feet. Algae make the bottom viscous at certain points. I move forward, dreading the insidious pressure of the current as cold takes over my legs and belly and trunk.

Standing on the far bank, Olio watches me as I painfully climb up. He is giggling, soaked and covered in goosebumps. Close by, there are some large flat stones heated by the sun.

We lie down on them to dry off. In the tall grass, a great blue heron observes us with one eye.

Is the river we have to cross to get to your camp like this one? Olio asks.

No, it's much wider. You need a canoe. When we get there, we'll whistle three times. That's the signal. You'll see, someone will come and get us.

I smile, lying in the noonday sun. My skin breathes. The wind moves over my body. I drift off to sleep, convinced it cannot be any other way. Olio will join me with my family.

When I open my eyes, the sun has changed position. It is three fifteen and Olio is nowhere to be seen. I jump up and look around. I call him, pulling on my clothes. The rumbling of the nearby rapids covers my voice. I start walking along the bank, worried, but my concern disappears when I catch sight of him at the foot of a series of pools. He is talking with a man who is fly-fishing. The silk of his line wheels and curves through the air, then delicately drops onto the still water.

When he notices me, Olio points me out to the fisherman. He slowly reels in his line and motions me over. When I come near, he looks me over from head to toe before offering his hand. His grip is vigorous, his eyes alert. Under his droopy, wide-brimmed hat, his hair is completely white.

Your younger brother told me all about it, he begins.

Really? I answer carefully.

The city in winter. I can't even imagine it. The big buildings with no lights, the cars abandoned, people stealing food. You're lucky to be in the woods now.

I nod and search out Olio's eyes. He is staring at the whirlpools in the river, sitting next to the man's creel.

We have a camp farther upstream, he says, adjusting the suspenders of his waders. You might not believe me, but I'm one of the youngest of the group. Unlike you, we didn't come to escape the blackout, we set up shop here a few years before. Far from everybody, far from the old folks' homes. My friends would be happy to see a boy your brother's age, but it's not a good time. We buried one of our colleagues this morning. We came out here to die, but you never get used to saying farewell to someone.

My sympathies, I say.

Olio comes back to us with a mischievous look that seems out of place, considering the conversation. The old man recovers his composure, leans over, hands on his thighs, and asks him if he knows how to work a rod and reel. Olio shakes his head. The fisherman tells us the salmon are late coming upriver this year, but if you're patient, you can catch some very nice trout.

The sun has crossed the treetops. The man notices the lengthening shadows as well. He needs to get back to his group and prepare the three fish he caught. He advises us to get back on the road again, showing me the opening to the path that cuts through the woods. His hand trembles as he points it out.

If you turn right at the foot of the second climb, you'll end up crossing a road. Like I was telling your younger brother, to get to the coast, all you have to do is follow it and you'll hit the access route that crosses the Park. With or without a vehicle, it's the shortest way to the sea.

The old man waves goodbye and turns away. We walk in silence, following his instructions. A little farther on, I ask Olio what he told the fisherman. His eyes triumphant, he opens his bag halfway. Three fine-looking trout are lying there. I look him in the eye.

We have enough supplies. You don't need to steal an old man's catch.

He gave them to me, he promises, just before you showed up.

7:50 P.M.

At the edge of the underbrush, we spot a dark shape moving heavily through the trees. We give it time to disappear into the bushes before continuing. We still haven't come across the road the fisherman told us about. I'm starting to have my doubts. Maybe he made up the story to steer us away from his place. We set up camp on the orange carpet of a pine forest and grill Olio's trout over the fire. Tree trunks stand as straight as soldiers all around us. We eat in silence, keeping watch over the shadows, with the smell of grilled fish and the bear prowling not far off.

The next day, we walk over four hours, then take a break to get oriented. It is twelve thirty. The air is heavy and sweat feels like slugs crawling across my skin. Still no sign of a road anywhere. I pull out the map and compass. Olio stands at my side. I study the topography lines and realize we are not at all where I thought.

I knew we shouldn't have believed that old man, Olio mutters, then takes the compass from my hand.

Why didn't you say anything?

When I'm told to follow, I follow, he retorts.

His remark gets on my nerves, and I try to take back my compass. But Olio has a firm grip on it. I grab him by the shoulder. When he feels my hand closing over him, he slips away, picks up a handful of needles, and throws them in my face. When I open my eyes, he has disappeared into the forest.

I curse, pack up my things, and go after him.

I hurry and manage to catch up to him farther on, at the opening to a clearing.

Give me back my compass.

He looks at me and raises his eyebrows. I insist. A sneaky look comes over his face. Something in me gives into his charm. I start laughing.

What are you two doing here? a voice rings out above our heads.

We jump.

Up there, Olio tells me.

A young woman is sitting motionless on a platform fastened to a tree, a rifle in her hands. She gives us a hostile look, then a few seconds later, climbs down.

I could have shot both of you, she tells us. I mean, if you were game.

We were just passing through, I say. Sorry to bother you.

She sizes me up from head to toe, then it's Olio's turn. The girl is a few years older than he is. She looks down her nose at him.

All right, she decides. Let's go, I'll follow you.

Where to?

With the business end of her rifle, she points across the clearing, where a little house and a rundown shed stand, like two phantom vessels anchored at the back of a bay.

We move through the stagnant air. The heat weighs upon us and the light is dazzling. The grass sticks to our pants. A second woman is sitting on the steps of the house, surrounded by five or six cats. She watches us come towards her. No reaction at first; then she gets up slowly and steps out of the shade. The cats come with her, wrapping themselves around her ankles.

Are you hurt? she asks, pointing to my leg.

I limp, that's all.

What are you doing here?

I look at her carefully, forgetting about the rifle pointed at my back. The little ropes of muscle along her shoulders and arms, her skin darkened by the sun, her nails encrusted with earth, her round belly, her heavy breasts.

We're going to the coast, Olio answers before I have a chance to come up with something.

On foot? she wonders, looking at our split-open boots.

That's the best means of transportation, I tell her, even when you limp.

Put down the rifle, the pregnant woman orders the younger one. I said put down your rifle. You'll have to excuse my sister's manners.

We've had a lot of visitors since last fall, her sister explains. And I'm not even talking about the guys with the shaved heads.

The pregnant woman motions her not to say anything more, then gauges our reaction. Like it or not, we're two guys who showed up out of the woods, lost, stunned, a couple of hallucinations. All the same, she invites us into the shade. We sit down at an old picnic table near a very large, fenced-in garden. The shed that offers us shade is about to fall to pieces. Brambles and wild vines climb the lacework of its boards, hang on to the vertical supports, and spill over the eaves. The house is in better shape, despite the boarded-up windows, the twisted roof shingles, and the mushrooms as big as LPs clinging to the wooden porch. Between the two buildings, sheets are drying on a line stretched between two trees.

So then, the older woman asks, sitting down, why are you going to the coast?

Olio glances at me, then tells her that airplanes go there.

Airplanes? the younger one interrupts. There hasn't been a plane in the sky for over a year!

We saw some, Olio claims.

Impossible. We would have heard them, we would have seen their trails in the sky.

Ask my cousin, Olio replies, pointing at me, his eyes sparkling.

The sisters turn to me. Olio won't give up his act. The vise is closing on me.

They weren't exactly planes from an airline company, I tell them.

Olio smiles discreetly, happy I'm making up stories with him. Then he goes off to explore the garden.

The older woman isn't convinced. The younger one lifts her eyes in search of long white vapour trails above our heads. The silence is heavy. The cats wander among us and rub against the leather of our boots. The older woman gives me a polite smile, gets up, holding her belly, and disappears on the other side of the cottony wall of the clothesline.

We admire the garden rows carefully separated by straw. Flowers and young vegetables stand out against the powerful green of tomato plants, zucchini, string beans, beets, potatoes, and leeks. The promise of this garden is magnificent. The younger woman watches our every move. When my eyes come to rest on the system of pipes that run from the rain barrels by the shed, she points out that they are her idea. She and her sister got tired of carrying water from the stream morning and night.

Now, it's easy. To water the garden, I just have to work the pump a few minutes.

From the corner of my eye, I spot Olio sneaking off behind the shed. Time to ask my question.

What's this business about people with shaved heads?

They must be camped somewhere around here, she answers, serious, because they would come around often. But then they understood.

Your sister, I say, changing my tone, is she going to give birth soon?

That's what it looks like, doesn't it?

Are you going to stay here?

We've always lived here, she says drily. It's our parents' house.

I question her with raised eyebrows.

They're having a nap. And you, she goes on, pointing her rifle at my pack, are you really going to the coast?

Before I can answer, the older sister returns with a bunch of radishes, some rhubarb stalks, and two jars of pickled cabbage.

This is for you. For the road. Just follow the path from here. A few kilometres and it'll hit the access route. Otherwise, you have everything you need?

Yes, I tell them, about to call Olio, things should be all right, thanks.

A cat gives a cry of pain and shoots out of the old shed. Olio appears a few seconds later. The girl shoots daggers at him. Olio smiles foolishly, then walks up to her to get his bag from under the table. She stands up, wanting to keep her distance. Ammunition falls from her back pocket. Olio picks it up, wheels around, hands it to her, and moves off with his arms stretched forward, making a motor noise with his mouth.

I say goodbye to the two young women, express our gratitude, then move off. When we go by the house, I look through the half-open door. A gas can stands on the kitchen table.

The younger one calls to me.

When you reach the passageway, cross over through the stream.

How come? Olio shouts back. Is it rotten?

No. We booby-trapped it.

We lose sight of them as we move along the path. It makes a long, lazy curve under the intense green of the trees. Again I am struck by how opaque the vegetation is, then I stumble over Olio, who stopped without warning.

Look, he says, pointing to a space set off by the edge of the trail.

Beneath the trees, there are two mounds of earth with wooden crosses and flowers. Then, off to one side, another mound. No crosses or flowers on that one.

Olio looks up at me.

Why did they booby-trap the bridge?

I think they rather not have visitors.

Later, we ford the stream as we were told to. As I splash through the water, I study the small log structure covered with earth. I don't see anything unusual. The logs aren't half-sawed through, there are no sharpened pikes hidden underneath, no detonator attached to the approach. But you never know.

My mother didn't like visitors either, Olio says as we finish crossing the stream. At night she jammed the cabin door shut with the back of a chair.

5:00 P.M.

The good weather of the last few days gives way to rain at the end of the afternoon. Water beats the leaves and slides down the bark. Fat drops fall from the underbrush. The humidity and grey skies soon get the better of us, and we hang my tarp between four trees for shelter.

With dry pine branches broken off from the bottom of a tree and some birchbark, Olio lights a fire a few steps from our position. The flames rise, sputtering in the rain. The light hypnotizes us; the smoke rises and turns. We eat the radishes and pickled cabbage that the two sisters gave us, then stretch out, keeping an eye on the puddles of water that have formed on the tarp. Darkness fills in the spots between the trees. Olio falls asleep. My body relaxes and fits into the knotty roots beneath my back. But I am awake. I listen to the rain pouring down on the forest. Olio mutters in his sleep. I flick on my lighter and look at the time. Twenty-five after midnight. Now and again, a branch drops a trail of water onto the tarp. A quarter to one. The rain eases up, each drop distinct from the others. One thirty in the morning. Mosquitoes buzz around my ears. Olio is restless; he talks in his sleep but I can't make out what he is saying, his words run together and night swallows his voice. I think of the wet grass waiting for us tomorrow. Then suddenly he lifts his head in a state of confusion.

We were in a bush plane! He is gasping for breath. The motor was roaring, and out the little window we could see the coast, the rocky capes, the wind turbines! Then something happened, a mechanical problem, turbulence, I'm not sure, the pilot was speaking another language, I didn't understand what she was saying, then the plane started diving straight towards the black spruce.

It's all right, I tell him gently, it's nothing, just a bad dream.

Olio stares at me as if I were speaking a foreign language, too. He shrugs, then tries to revive the fire by blowing on it. Miraculously, it springs to life. I check my watch. Twenty after two.

Olio moves closer to the flames, rummages through his pockets, and takes out a bullet, turning it every which way.

What are you doing with that?

His back is towards me, but I can imagine his sly grin. I picture him wheeling around yesterday afternoon with the girl's ammunition in his hand.

Why did you take that? What do you want to do with it?

I don't know, he admits. I just wanted to try. And it worked.

The flames whistle as they bite into the wood, then rise into the night. Olio is sitting cross-legged. I watch him and again I wonder why he is with me.

That's enough now. Tell me what happened to you.

He draws out the silence a little more.

In the fall, my father left for the coast to get the rest of our supplies. The roads are still passable, he said, it's now or never. But he never came back. To keep the stove going during the winter, my mother looked for dead wood in the forest. I guess she hoped my father would walk out from behind a tree, because every time, she came back with frozen tears on her cheeks. One time, my brother and I went with her, and we saw people. They were moving along the mountainside with heavy packs on their backs. I shouted so they would hear us. My mother shushed me and we turned back without picking up our usual load of wood. When we got inside, she blocked the door with the back of a chair. She was swearing at me.

Olio presses his lips together. His eyes blink in the darkness. He can't continue.

Then what happened? I ask to urge him on. Why aren't you with your mother and your brother? Where are they?

My salvo of questions rings through the forest. Olio freezes like a frightened animal. He opens his hand and drops the ammunition into the fire.

I throw myself on him and flatten him against the ground. Seconds later, a fiery ball of incandescent light explodes in the night. My ears ring from the explosion. My face is covered in wet ash. The fire is blown apart, the embers scattered. Olio gets up slowly with a satisfied look.

I am beside myself.

What the hell came over you? The thing could have gone in our direction, it could have blown up, you could have killed us.

I go back to my sleeping spot. No sense saying more. My heartbeat is pounding in my ears. The kid is crazy. The rain slowly drowns the constellation of scattered embers. Dying stars floating in the darkness. Olio curls up near me and immediately falls asleep. I am awake, wondering what I am going to do with him. I feel his warm breath against my back, the night weighs heavily, and the belly of the tarp sags.

6:55 A.M.

Morning breaks in full sunshine. We head out early and finally hook up with the access road. Some tire tracks on the wet surface, the puddles are murky, but there is no one around.

I watch Olio zigzagging down the road. It's like he's searching for something to see or do, as if walking down a flat straight path wasn't enough for him. I think of the supplies he got his hands on, my compass in his pocket, the bullet he threw into the fire last night. I don't know what kind of game he is playing. I tried to ask about his mother earlier and he completely ignored me. I believe that in one way or another, Olio will end up telling his story, opening up, revealing himself. I will get the best of him sooner or later.

A grasshopper jumps out in front of him. He hunts it down, chasing it like a crafty young lion, from the side. When he comes up close to his prey, he leaps and lands on it with both feet, then moves on, whistling. A few steps behind, I look down at the flattened insect. Its legs are still stirring. I put it out of its misery with my boot.

In mid-afternoon, we come to a fork. Out loud, Olio reads what is written on a peeling sign.

> Cottages available
> Rowboats for rent
> Twenty-five metres

From where we stand, we can make out a lake below. A long black line between two walls of straight trees. On the other side, the first summits of the Park. I take a quick look at the map. We will have to go around the lake on the road; there is no other choice.

Let's go, I say to Olio, heading out. We'll take the road.

When I look over my shoulder, a few minutes later, he is gone. I stop, sigh, and go back. I return to the turnoff, call his name, then move down the gravel drive towards the lake.

At the end, there are a few small houses and a little church. The buildings look well maintained, but the place is strangely deserted. I'm on the alert. Someone whistles off to my right. Olio. He motions me to follow and cut through the forest. I glance around, then fall in behind him. We come out onto a grassy point that thrusts into the lake. A soft breeze pushes small, sparkling waves onto the stones. The rhythm is slow and even. A few islands lie farther on, skinny clumps of earth covered with bent birch and black spruce.

We shouldn't stay here, I warn him.

He drops his bag, then his clothes, and jumps into the water. He tells me to do the same. I refuse.

Look, there's nobody, he insists, the lake is ours.

I listen hard. Nothing. Just the high-pitched voice of a kid at play. A dragonfly lands nearby. Its bright colours stand out against the deep green of the plants. The lake is reflected in the globes of its eyes. Olio tries to splash me and wants to know what I'm waiting for. The dragonfly moves on, buzzing as it heads into the sky. Finally, my hands loosen on my walking sticks.

I take off my clothes, cross the slimy bottom, and dive into the lake's undulating reflection. The sun has warmed the surface, but it is cold deeper down. The temperature difference awakens every scratch on my body. Olio swims over to me, beating his legs hard. He moves in wide circles, dives below the surface, and reappears, yelling, a few centimetres from my face. He laughs, swims away again, then floats on his back. I try and do the same, but sink like a stone as soon as I stop moving.

How did you learn to swim?

Like everybody else, he replies, splashing me. My father threw me into the water and I figured out how to get back to land.

We have a water fight and chase each other for a while, then swim lazily back towards the shore. When we touch bottom, the muck slips between our toes, the water turns murky, and our feet sink in. Olio laughs at the viscous bubbles breaking the surface. I look at the grassy point. The sun is high. Everything is calm, and our things are still there. I gaze at the mountains and try to visualize the long road that circles the lake. If, by magic, we could get to the other side, we would save a couple days' walking.

A piece of silty earth hits my shoulder and pulls me from my thoughts. The muck runs down my body. Laughter reaches up to the sky. I bend down and gather a handful of wet sand. Olio dodges my shot. Triumphant, he dashes into the shallow water.

Try again, he challenges me.

His steps leave traces on the surface like a ricocheting pebble. My next shot curves high into the air and misses my target by a mile. Olio moves farther away, out of reach, and disappears on the far side of the point. I watch the forest that circles the lake and my vigilance returns. Olio returns to bombard me with birdshot that breaks up in the air and falls into the water. We decide to declare a truce. The burning sun beats down on us. The temperature is rising. I ask him what is on the other side. He shrugs.

A wooden dock with rowboats.

I tell him it's time to leave. He protests, then follows me, the strap of his bag across his forehead.

We could go have a look in the church, he says dreamily.

A few steps later, I hear rustling at the edge of the woods. Hidden in the leaves, a dozen kids are spying on us. Their eyes shine in the shadows. I wonder what to do. Maybe we'd be better off taking the road along the shore. Olio solves the issue by raising his arms and shouting. The kids run off like panicked, awkward animals.

The coast is clear, he declares, stepping in front of me.

We get to the gravel drive, moving quickly. After the first curve, a group of men intercepts us. The sun glistens off their smooth skulls. Olio slips behind me.

Are you lost? one of them asks.

No, I tell him, trying to figure out if they are armed, we just stopped for a swim.

We stand there, eyeing each other.

Come with us, the guy says sharply.

He steps forward with his group. I don't think they are armed, but Olio and I do as we're told. It is eleven o'clock by the time we reach the little buildings at the end of the drive. Summer cottages, all the same, painted sky blue, with a shed and a few flowers in front. At the door of each cottage, men, women, and children watch us go past, their eyes wide. They have their hair cut short, too. The sun casts the shadow of the church steeple on the ground before us. A wide set of stairs leads to a dock where boats are tied up. We are escorted to the entrance of one of the cottages.

What is this about? a voice calls from inside.

Hikers, one of the men answers. I figure they're going to the Station.

Send them in. You guys can stand down.

Olio and I stay on the porch.

Come in.

We step inside. The cool air is a surprise after the heat. A man with long hair comes over. His voice is deep and echoes within the walls of his house.

We knew it would happen, and we were ready. Now that all the lights have gone out and the whole world is dissolving and looking for a reason to exist, there are more and more of us prepared for what will come next. And you? Are you ready?

Olio and I notice the man's erratic gaze. His pupils move in different directions and stop at times, staring into emptiness.

You want to cross the Park, right?

Yes.

You've done well to choose the forest, he says, but you're not going to the right place.

You don't know anything about us, Olio tells him coolly.

And you two, the man answers, what do you know about each other?

Olio turns. I let him know it's time to leave. The church bells are ringing. The man insists. We have come at the right time, meal time, there's no use refusing, we are his guests.

The next minute, we hear an uproar as dozens of adults and children emerge from the cottages and cross the drive in front of us.

Don't be shy, he tells us, you're hungry and the table is set.

We join the small crowd at the old picnic tables in the shade of tall poplars. People come and talk to the long-haired man and take a closer look at us. Talk continues at the tables as we are served a trout fillet with sauerkraut. Olio quickly takes a few bites. That earns us a shocked stare from the assembly.

Our host gets to his feet and the buzz of conversation fades.

Today we are joined by two hikers. May our food help them see clearly in this dark world.

When he sits down again, everyone digs into their meal.

I suppose you met the two women living alone not far from here, the man begins.

The two sisters? Olio asks.

You can thank your lucky stars you're still alive, a guy tells us from the next table. They shot at us every time we tried to help them. They killed one of ours for no reason last fall.

They don't believe in anything, our host mutters.

The older one is pregnant, I say.

A look of discomfort runs across their faces.

We'll have to go back there, the guy from the other table concludes.

Olio glances at me. In his eyes I can see the bridge that the two sisters booby-trapped. Our host listens to our silence, but says no more.

When the meal is over, everyone rises at once. They clear the tables and go on their way. A group of kids are the only ones left. They go over to Olio and ask him to play. He looks in my direction.

Let him do what he wants, the man tells me, pushing back his long hair.

I drum my fingers on the table as Olio joins the little crowd. The afternoon vibrates with heat, the lake throws off turquoise reflections, and the aluminum rowboats shine from their wooden dock.

See how good our lives are here? The man's voice is so calm it gets on my nerves. That boy has something special. You can feel it. Why are you going to the Station? You could stay with us, you know.

I look at my watch, thank him, and get to my feet. We have a long way to go before nightfall.

I won't stop you, he pursues. Get back on the road if that will make you feel like you're getting somewhere. But are you sure the young man wants the same thing you do?

I keep my anger inside.

Olio returns. I can read a mad plan on his face. He takes my hand and pulls me hurriedly towards the dock. The kids watch us, amazed, as we climb into a rowboat. We row with all our might, surprised that no one comes to chase after us. The boat pulls to one side as we leave the shore in choppy fashion. The long-haired man steps onto the dock with the kids. The lake is so clear we can see leaches undulating on the slimy bottom.

If you see the Park warden, the man calls, his two hands a megaphone, tell him we'll be coming to visit him soon.

We coordinate our rowing the best we can. We reach the other shore a half-hour later, relieved when the little settlement is no more than a rosary of blue pearls in the spiny green landscape. And we are happy, too, to have spared ourselves a long detour, and to be heading directly into the woods with the mountains of the Park as our guide.

3:20 P.M.

At least the long-haired guy was right about one thing. Walking makes you feel like you're getting somewhere. Since yesterday, we've been walking through the woods with greater confidence. According to the map, when we cross the main road again, we will practically be at the Park entrance.

Often, Olio moves on ahead of me. I lose sight of him sometimes in the maw of the forest, then find him later on, sitting on a rock or perched on a tree branch. But this time he is nowhere to be seen; it's been two hours. I step up my pace and try to catch up to him.

He can't be very far.

The vegetation is sparse, and slender white birch push up between giant decomposing stumps covered with spongy moss. An old clear-cut zone where the vegetation is growing back patiently, stubbornly, on the humus of a forest that has disappeared.

A rustling in the bushes. I jump.

Is that you, Olio?

No answer.

Olio?

The foliage shivers.

That's enough, come out.

I hesitate. Maybe it's just a little animal. Unless it's a bear. I move on, whistling to show I'm here. The feeling of being followed persists, but walking calms me. When the sound starts up again behind me, my heart races and I wheel around, my sticks raised. Olio. A wide smile on his face.

Still scared of wild beasts?

I breathe out, furious but relieved. At the end of the day, we come to the access road, deserted and lined with tall grass. We kick up gravel and send a hare running. Above, the mountains of the Park thrust out their chests.

A little farther on, the road is choked with smashed vehicles. They lie in the sun like carcasses picked over by scavengers. Olio climbs into the labyrinth of glass and metal leading towards the arch that marks the Park entrance. I move around the obstacle, examining the vehicles, but it looks like they have been completely looted. I recognize the Jeep that belonged to the guys we helped out ten days ago or so. I notice a minibus lying on its side with skis in front and caterpillar tracks in back. This ark built for winter gives me a strange feeling. It has come to rest amid the brambles and wild wheat. I catch up to Olio at the entrance. The gate that blocks the way is solid steel. It is bent and dented, but has not given way. A vandalized information panel hangs on the wall of the little shelter.

Hello? Olio calls.

His voice joins the ungraspable chant of the insects and is lost in the late afternoon air. We go towards the welcome booth. Its doors and windows are barricaded. I circle it, hoping to find a way to break in. There must be vending machines inside. Maybe even something left in them. It wouldn't be bad to have extra supplies before crossing the Park. Using one of my walking sticks as a lever, I try to pry off the plywood sheet covering the door. No use. I'll only break my stick.

I sit down on my pack and gaze at the mountains of the Park. Tall pines stretch their arms above the forest, as if they were about to take a swan dive. Olio has captured a salamander and is playing with it in his rough way. I tell him to leave it alone.

Six p.m. has come and gone, and the light has taken on an orange glow. I figure it's better to spend the night here, by the shelter, and leave tomorrow morning. Just then, loud barking tears apart the peacefulness of day's end. A big black dog rushes out of the woods and heads straight towards us. I jump to my feet and stand in front of Olio, using my pack as a shield. The animal moves on us, yapping, its fur on end. As I look for something to throw at it, a man steps out of the shadows and whistles between his teeth. The dog stops and stares at us with its bug eyes, then wants to be petted, slobber and all.

What are you doing here? the man asks, coming up to us.

He must be in his sixties, thin and wearing a green cap with the yellow logo of a tractor company on it. He inspects us coldly. In a holster at his belt is a pair of clippers, or maybe a revolver. He is clearly wary of us.

Look, says Olio, going straight to the man, I found a salamander. It's black and red. Pretty, isn't it?

The man's shoulders loosen, and he bends over to examine the creature.

It's beautiful, he says, then raises his eyes to me. I'm the warden here, but as you can see, everything is closed down now.

I nod.

You're going to the Station, is that it?

No, I tell him, we want to cross the Park.

We're going to the coast, Olio puts in. They've got electricity there.

The man pats his dog on the head, doubtful about Olio's claim.

How can you be so sure?

By going there, he replies.

The guard allows himself a smile.

You've got a long way to go to get to the coast, but if you cross the Park, you'll reach it sooner or later. They might have electricity there, with the wind turbines.

He stops, his thoughts elsewhere. His emaciated face is strangely familiar.

Here, when we heard talk about the blackout, he goes on, nobody believed it. But since we didn't receive any directives, my colleagues all left, first one, then the other. But someone had to stay behind to close the gate.

In disbelief, I contemplate the traffic jam of ghost vehicles in the middle of the forest.

Then I recognize him. It's Luperc, my aunt Hesta's husband. I never saw much of him because he was always in the woods. He has changed a lot, his face has sagged, his shoulders are stooped, but it's him all right. When I say his name, light flashes in his eyes. He knows who I am.

I thought you were at the other end of the country! he says, astonished. Hesta never told me you had a son. You two make a handsome pair, that's for sure!

I quickly describe how I met Olio, but Luperc is so enthusiastic he pays no attention and gives me a hearty hug. He can't believe I spent the winter in the village. And, even more incredible, that I'm on my way, on foot, to my family's camp.

Now that I think about it, that makes more sense than the coast, he jokes. Come on, you must be starving. Come with me.

Olio drops the salamander like it was a meaningless object and falls in behind Luperc, down a path bordered on both sides by impressive stacks of firewood. At the end is a mobile home, practically brand new, set on concrete blocks. Four sheet-metal walls, a door in the middle, two sash windows. If it weren't for the rocking chair on the little porch, you might think the place was a bunker. On one side are large tree trunks ready to be split.

We go into the trailer. A smell of cigarette smoke clings to the walls, and dirty dishes fill the sink. A big pot sits on the gas stove. The dog slips between our legs, goes around the table, slurps a little water, then disappears into a back room. Shafts of late afternoon light enter the kitchen and striate the stagnant blue air of the kitchen.

Luperc serves us a generous portion of stew. The carrots are good with the meat and brown sauce, and the smell makes our mouths water. We thank him as we wolf down our rations.

It's Hesta's recipe, he tells us, lighting a cigarette.

Where is she? Olio wants to know, his mouth full.

Luperc turns to me.

Hesta? At the camp. She decided to go with her brothers and sisters. We would have been happy here, the two of us.

Aren't you eating? Olio asks.

Later, maybe, Luperc tells him, pulling on his cigarette.

For a moment, it's like time has stopped. A wave of memories rises in me. My mother's gravestone, my father's self-imposed exile in the garage, the house too big, my aunt Hesta coming in every day to bring me the food she prepared.

I look at the clock on the wall. The second hand keeps hitting the same number, and it can't get the other hand to follow it.

What time is it? Luperc asks, pointing at my watch.

Seven twenty-five.

Luperc adjusts his clock, gives it a jolt, and the hands start their cycle again. Olio licks the bottom of his bowl, gets up, and finds a tennis ball on the floor. When he bounces it, the dog jumps up, wagging his tail.

Let's go out on the porch, Luperc suggests.

He carries a second chair outside and we sit and watch Olio playing ball with the dog that is barking happily. Evening settles over the forest. The air is mild. There are not too many mosquitoes. My belly is full. For the first time in a very long time, I relax.

At the beginning, Luperc begins, a lot of people came down from the Park. Hikers and tourists in rental cars. I still hadn't gotten any news from head office. I wanted to pull out of here, too. But where would I go? I knew Hesta wouldn't be in the village, waiting for me. Then, from the kitchen window, I saw the first convoy. Three or four vehicles together. I went out to see them. They wanted to go to the Station. I tried to explain that everything was closed; they didn't want to listen. The next day they left on foot, and their cars stayed here. Then more people showed up. Some of them tried to force the gate. Others looted the welcome booth. At first I sent my dogs, but one of them got shot. Now I don't go down there except to search the vehicles. With everything people left behind, I find all that I need. Even coffee and cigarettes!

He pulls off his cap and runs his hand over his forehead.

It's good to have a little visit. Except for the people passing the gate, there's just the shaved-head guys who come prowling around. And believe me, you don't want to have anything to do with them. I've got no idea what's happening at the Station. The radio went down with the blackout. Strange, because everything is supposed to work on its own over there. In any case, if you want to cross the Park, my advice is to take the paths and avoid the valley where the Station is. It's longer, but safer. With a little luck, you'll have good weather.

That's what we had in mind, Olio speaks up, coming to join us.

Luperc chuckles. Your boy is quite the number, he says.

Then he talks about the weather, and how he came to work for the Park when he was twenty-five, and how moose stick their noses in his windows, and he points to the trees he intends to cut down soon. Night moves over the forest. Olio falls asleep, his head on my legs, lulled by the comforting sound of our voices.

You can have my room, Luperc offers. I sleep on the sofa, anyway.

I pick up Olio in my arms and carry him to the bed. The dog comes in, too, climbs on the mattress, then curls up in a ball next to him. When I go back out onto the porch, the moon is rising above the rugged outline of the Park, casting pale, white light over the endless stacks of firewood along the path.

You've got enough for the next ten winters, I tell him, curious.

You've got to keep yourself busy, Luperc explains, producing a flask from his pocket.

We take a pull or two. The heat of the alcohol warms my heart.

Why don't you come to the camp with us?

Luperc's face darkens.

I don't know if you remember, but I never got along with Hesta's brothers. Especially Darès. I don't think I'd be welcome. Anyway, I'd rather work things out on my own. In peace. It's not the same for you, he adds, trying to reassure me. You're part of the family.

I think of my uncle Darès. It's true, he's obstinate. The oldest of the brothers. Diane is the only one not afraid to stand up to him. Her and Boccus, sometimes.

Luperc changes the subject, and asks me about the condition of the roads. I tell him some won't be passable very much longer. Not to mention the roadblocks. He listens, frowns, and turns his face towards the density of the forest.

The night lasts until we have emptied his flask and smoked the rest of his cigarettes.

The next morning, Olio and I awake with the dawn. Luperc is already on his feet. He is sipping coffee and looking out the kitchen window.

I fixed you some supplies. You'll be able to hold out for a while. And I'd like you to give something to your aunt Hesta for me, he says, handing me a letter folded in four.

After breakfast, we thank Luperc and put our packs on our backs. I wriggle around until mine is balanced. The extra supplies make it heavier.

You'll see, Luperc tells us, keeping his dog close by his side, the path is well marked. There are shelters every twenty kilometres or so. And the view is magnificent from the mountaintops.

I promise I'll deliver his letter. His eyes light up a moment; then he turns evasive. He kicks a stone and watches it skitter across the grass. The breeze lifts his thinning hair.

Everything is closed down here, he explains, swallowing back his tears, but I'm still keeping watch. Tell your aunt I'm here, I'm not going anywhere, and ... I'm thinking of her. Go ahead now, it's time to leave, I've got wood to split.

We say goodbye to him and go past the meticulously stacked cords of wood, then the tangle of abandoned vehicles and the Park gate. Before us, the peaks hide a wide swath of the sky. Olio leads the way, wearing a yellow-and-green cap. Soon the echo of an axe splitting wood rings through the forest, and then it is swallowed up by the mountains.

NOON

We move farther into the Park. The ascents are steep, and the descents cross escarpments and rivers raging deep in the valleys. Except for a few trees that have fallen over winter, the trail network is still in good shape. Narrow bridges give us passage over streams, stone stairways make certain grades easier, signage directs us along the path, and wooden lookouts have been built to admire the landscape. Every night, we sleep in shelters, exceedingly simple in their construction. Four walls, a roof, and two wooden sleeping platforms. The cool air and the mosquitoes slip through the planks, but at least we stay dry.

The days of walking are like steps one after the other, the landscapes blend together, we meet no one. The Park trails are long, green corridors, and if it were not for the rustling of animals that slip away as soon as they sense our presence, we would feel alone in the world.

Later, Olio waits for me near a little marsh where tall grass and cattails gather around trees that have died standing up.

It was night, he begins, his eyes lost in the distance, the cabin door was open. I thought of the chair jammed against the knob and I didn't understand how that could have happened. Why I didn't wake up. The cold had crawled into our beds. I called my mother once, twice, three times. My little brother woke up crying. I reassured him the best I could, I told him our mother had gone out for some fresh air.

I made a fire, I cooked some soup, I waited. Then I waited some more. In the morning, there were just ashes in the stove and the soup was cold. I dressed my little brother to go outside. The snow was all stamped down by the front door. People had been there. The footsteps went into the forest. We followed them until night fell. My little brother was whimpering. We had to go back. We spent the rest of the winter in the cabin, rationing our supplies, praying that our parents would return and that everything would go back to how it was before.

That's a horrible story, I say, shocked.

Olio sniffs. I try to comfort him. I understand him. I know the weight of winter, and even if part of me is not so sure about his story, I share his distress.

As I put a hand on his shoulder, a beaver breaks the surface between the water lilies and slaps the water with its tail to scare us. Olio jumps, backs off, and picks up his bag, muttering, as if he had been caught in the act.

We stop a little while later to eat on a summit rounded down by wind and water. It is high noon and the heat crushes us with its glaring light. The spot is covered with yellow grass, scraggly bushes, and a scattering of violet flowers. Birds of prey criss-cross the sky. We lean against a rock to nibble on some dry crackers and flakes of ham. The slope in front of us dives head first into a patchwork of trees and streams.

Olio watches me drink the juice of the canned ham. I turn and wipe off the drops hanging from my moustache.

We'd better get going, I tell him, an eye on the clouds building up on the horizon. It's looking like rain.

Let's go, he mocks me, imitating my voice, it's looking like rain.

We begin the descent along a ridge line. On each side, wide valleys open up the landscape.

At the end of the day, we reach a shelter as clouds take

over the sky. Inside, we do exactly what we did the previous nights. We put down our packs, breathing hard, we pull off our boots, light a candle, sit facing each other, then have dinner as we evaluate the next day's route on the map. When we lie down on our wooden beds, the birds, insects, and creatures of the night have all fallen silent. Nothing but the wind shaking the tree branches and the rain that has started to fall.

Olio calls my name. He is holding a small object.

Look what I found under the bed.

His voice breaks the spell of sleep that had begun to come over me. I rub my eyes and lift my head. He is holding a digital camera. He tries to turn it on but the screen stays black.

It's broken for sure, I say.

Olio will have none of it. He takes the batteries from my headlamp and puts them into the camera. Bluish light fills the room.

Come here.

I sit by his side, half asleep, half curious. The first image emerges from the darkness like the memory of a distant time.

A couple and three children are crowded in front of the lens. The man holds the camera as far back as possible. Their smiles glow and the mountains are a pastel colour in the background. The picture looks like an advertisement for happy families.

Olio jumps to the next photo. The woman is walking down a path with the children. Her hair is carefully tied back, the frames of her glasses shine in the sun, and her fleece vest is slightly open over her breasts.

The next picture is dark. The man is kneeling in front of a fire, looking at the camera. The logo of his fashionable outdoor clothing is visible. On the ground, I can make out a few packets of dried food, a GPS, and mosquito repellant.

Quite the contrast with my worn-out boots, dirty pants, and patched-up pack.

Where are these people now? Olio asks, scrolling through the photos faster and faster.

I shrug. His eyes fill with tears. He pulls the batteries out of the device and the mirage of the past fades.

And your little brother, I venture, where is he now?

Olio looks away, cocks his arm, and throws the camera against the wall. The pieces scatter across the floor.

Now it's broken for sure, he declares.

I hide my consternation, and decide not to react to the boy's impulsiveness. Gusts of wind rattle the door to the shelter as if someone were trying to get in.

Tell me about your aunts and uncles, Olio says.

The question comes as a surprise. I take a breath, clear my throat. The candle flame draws shadows on the ceiling.

My mother's brothers and sisters. They talk loud, they laugh hard, they play cards, they hunt, they work like the devil. I haven't seen them for a long time. But I imagine they haven't changed. First, there's Uncle Nep. He used to lend us a hand at the garage. The only one who got along with my father. There's Hesta, Luperc's wife, and the others: Herman, Boccus, Diane, Darès. They used to take me to the camp with them. In the spring to open it, in the summer to maintain the trails, in the fall to go hunting. Every time I left, my father would get pissed off because he was losing two pairs of hands.

What if there's no one at the camp? Olio interrupts.

Impossible.

But if it was true, where would we go?

Rain beats the roof and gusts of wind howl darkly. Olio is impatient. He takes out the map.

I know where. Right here, he points.

I lean over to look. A violent gust of wind throws the

door open, scatters the map, and casts us into darkness. Olio goes to shut the door as I feel for my lighter.

I hear a voice, he says, listening to the storm.

It's just the wind. Close the door so I can light the candle.

No, for real. Come and listen.

It's late. I get to my feet awkwardly and go to the threshold. The wind is pounding the rain to the ground. Water streams everywhere. The leaves wave wildly. A herd of invisible animals stampeding through the forest.

It's the wind, what else could it be?

Then, a moment later, I sense something behind the uproar of the storm. I am skeptical, but when it starts up again, there's no doubt. Someone is calling for help.

MIDNIGHT

Olio takes a step or two into the darkness. The wind whips his clothes. Raindrops are loud on the foliage. A ray of light pierces the darkness.

Should we go? he asks, adjusting my headlamp on his forehead.

Rain sweeps away the light. Leaves tremble. Treetops wave and bang together. We walk through the black, troubled forest, our necks bent, as if an anvil were weighing on our heads. The ground is spongy with water. Our feet sink into the mud. My knee sends pain signals and I regret not taking my sticks. We stop and listen but the downpour covers everything.

Hello! Olio calls through the megaphone of his hands.

No one answers. We're soaked already. Olio leaves the path and cuts through the woods. I'm not so sure that's a good idea. We could lose our way in the night. The trees all look the same.

I push my way forward, fighting the branches, then stumble over Olio, who has stopped. His light blinds me when he turns in my direction. Water pours down on our faces and runs into our half-open mouths. Olio turns and motions with his hand as the storm pauses briefly in its dance.

Hello! he calls again.

Here! We're over here!

The voice is whisked away by the wind.

We push our way through the trunks that shine in the

headlamp. Branches bend and crack above. Dead limbs fall all around us and break on the ground. Up ahead, we pick out two figures sheltered under the branch-work of a pine. A man and a woman. Olio casts his light on them as they emerge from their spot and come to us.

Thank you, thank you, the woman repeats. Thank you so much.

The man raises his hand to keep from being blinded by the beam.

There's a shelter not far from here, isn't there? Isn't there? he insists in a broken voice.

Yes, I tell him, a little taken aback. What are you doing here?

Before they can answer, I hear the cries of a baby from under the woman's coat.

Later, the man grumbles, we'll tell you later. Just take us to the shelter. Please.

Follow me, Olio tells them, starting out through the forest streaming with rain.

The two refugees fall in behind him. I bring up the rear and watch the man struggling under the weight of his pack. A flash of lightning reveals the sinister position of the trees around us. When the thunderclap follows a few seconds later, the man is startled and loses his footing on the muddy trail. I help him up as he curses his fate. We catch up to Olio and the woman.

It is exactly midnight when our little convoy reaches the shelter. We are soaked and stunned. The man throws off his pack and drops onto one of the wooden beds. The woman quickly unwraps the newborn from her scarf.

Here, she entreats me, take her a minute. Just tap her on the back a little, there's nothing to it.

I have no choice. I reach for the swaddling package that is screaming away and try to comfort her against my shoulder.

It is the first time I have held a child of that age. I do my best to stay calm, but my pulse starts to race. I rub her back, I rock her, I hum a tune. Nothing works. The wind circles our shelter like a mob of hungry beasts.

The woman takes out a first-aid kit from their bag and bends over the man to help him pull off his clothes. I am shocked to see his shirt soaked with blood. A deep wound glistens just above his collarbone. The man curses and complains as the woman examines him and disinfects everything with alcohol swabs.

You'll be all right, she sighs, then kisses him. The bullet went through without hitting the bone.

What happened? I ask over the noise of the sobbing baby.

The man sits, unmoving, one hand on his shoulder, his head thrown back. An acrid smell hangs in the air. A mix of humidity, sweat, dried blood, and the baby's urine. The woman turns and looks at me. Her wide eyes are red and exhausted.

We escaped the Station, she tells me as she bandages the man's wound, that's what happened.

The baby's cries fill the shelter. I can't seem to do anything about it. Olio wants me to give her to him. He wraps her in his golden cape and goes to sit with her in a corner. The baby immediately calms down. I go back to our refugees.

Fine, you escaped the Station. What's happening there?

The woman sighs heavily, then asks us to turn around, she wants to put on dry clothes. We obey and stare at the wooden wall. As she changes, wind skims the shelter and the candle flame wavers in the draft.

That's where we're going, Olio says to make them talk. We want to know!

Don't go there, the man warns, whatever you do. There's too many people, not enough resources, everyone's going crazy, it's total chaos.

The woman takes her daughter from Olio's arms, checks her cloth diaper, and gives her the breast.

I'd been working for the Park for three years, she says. When we heard about the blackout, we were in high season and much too busy to worry about it. Besides, everything runs on generators there. Even the tourists laughed at what they saw on the news. They kept going on their hikes, to the spa, the restaurant. But when the deliveries stopped and the satellite network broke down, it was panic. Vacation was over. Some people left. They fought over the vehicles and the gas that was left. Other people, like us, decided to stay right where we were. We figured we'd be safe from the world's madness.

After drinking her fill, the baby falls asleep against her mother's body.

At first, things went pretty well. We managed to divide up the jobs, share the space, go beyond the language barrier. There were about a hundred of us, but we had everything we needed. Even a few hours of electricity in the evening.

I realized I was pregnant in the fall, just before the first groups started showing up. Small numbers, families, most of them, who had abandoned their vehicles at one of the Park entrances and come up the access road on foot. Often they were ill-equipped, exhausted, starving. The nights were starting to get cold. We couldn't just leave them on their own. Then more of them started coming, more and more. When snow blocked the roads for good, all three hotels at the Station were beyond capacity.

By the end of the winter, the generators were out of gas and food was in short supply. Clans started forming, confusion had taken over, we didn't really know who was making the decisions. The baby was born in the middle of that, in the spring. With better weather, more people came streaming into the Station. By then, they had to make their own camps.

And if they wanted to stay, they had to bring back meat. Within a few weeks, the Station was covered with tents and the woods were filled with very eager hunters.

We didn't see how we could manage another winter there. Especially with the new baby. We decided to leave. But it's not that easy. Guards are posted all around the base. No one is allowed to take out material or food except to go hunting. We slipped out this morning at dawn, hoping to make it through the forest. But they spotted us just before we reached the line of trees.

They hunted us down like dogs, the man bursts out, his face distorted by pain.

The woman scolds him. If he keeps twisting and turning, the wound will never heal. I pass them some canned tuna and a pack of nuts. We eat in silence, listening to the howling of the wind and watching the clothes shed their water from the rafters.

When I think about it, the woman says, I can't believe you heard us in the storm. Where are you guys coming from?

Our plane crash-landed not far from here, Olio tells her.

Here we go again, I say to myself.

Your plane, really? the man says, incredulous, as he looks us over. You're in pretty good shape.

The storm rages and the air whistles through the boards of our shelter. It's like being in a fuselage in free fall through the sky.

We were lucky, I say to change the subject. The people with us were killed instantly.

Olio smiles as I build on his story. The conversation peters out. I look at my watch. Two fifteen in the morning. The man is tipping into sleep, his head heavy on this chest. We blow out the candle and darkness takes over. Olio lies on the floor near the packs. The rhythm of the rain and the branches scraping against the fragile frame of our shelter begin to hypnotize me. I am exhausted but can't sleep. A question haunts me.

Where will you go next?

We'll probably stay here a few days, the woman answers in a hushed voice, we have no choice. Afterward, we'll take the trails out of the Park. There's an old mining village farther on, in the backcountry. We know people there. We'll be able to rest up a bit. Afterward, we'll see.

It's striking, they are about to walk the same path I did. But in the other direction.

Do you have all you need?

We have the Park map with the trails and shelters, everything for the baby, and rations for ten days or so. That should do it.

I make a quick calculation. It's not enough. Spontaneously, I tell her to stop at the welcome centre and go see the guard.

Tell him I sent you. His name is Luperc. He'll help you, I'm sure he will. He's my uncle. He gave us supplies to cross the Park.

She thanks me, but there is distrust in her voice. I realize I have contradicted Olio's story about the plane.

We've been walking since the beginning, I admit, and look at Olio. His eyes are wide open and shine in the darkness.

Which reminds me, the woman says, there's a float plane at the Station. It belongs to the owners. It was supposed to be repaired, but with the blackout, it hasn't moved from its moorings on the river. No one wants to touch it. We're better off trusting our legs, right?

A terrible crash shakes the shelter like a sound box. A branch has fallen on the roof. The man sits bolt upright, gasps for breath, says something I can't make out, then falls back asleep. The baby wakes up, crying.

Everything's all right, her mother tells her, it's nothing.

I imagine the impact of a whole tree. The sheet-metal roof split open, the timbers twisted, night bursting in from above our heads. The woman sings a lullaby. Her voice fills the room. I know the tune. The baby is peaceful now. Even the storm seems quieter.

6:10 A.M.

Dawn pierces the cloud cover. The wind and the rain have stopped. Grey light slips through the cracks. Olio is sitting by my side, his bag on his knees. On the other bed, the woman is dressing her baby as the man inspects his wound.

After a quick breakfast, I take out some canned goods and offer them to the couple. They stare, surprised.

Take it, you'll need it.

They thank me. As I lace up my boots, they insist again. We should change our plans and avoid the Station. I nod.

Olio keeps the baby busy by making faces at her. When he gets ready to leave, the woman smiles. We're family, that's easy to see. It's our turn to laugh. We wish them good luck, then step out the door.

Mist hangs over the forest. Branches litter the ground and leaves are carried by the water running between endless knots of roots. Trees stripped by the wind lean one against the other, exhausted by last night's terrible dance. Olio leads the way. His footsteps push water from the ground. I pick up my sticks and venture into this disorderly landscape that the birds are beginning to restore with the brilliance of their songs.

We move into a cage of soaked vegetation, stepping over the heads of pine trees lopped off by the storm. Rain has turned the trail into a ravine. To keep the earth from sticking to the soles of our boots, making each step leaden, we try to put our feet on rocks laid bare by the water. We manoeuvre around groves of trees that have been knocked down. Broken roots stick out from mounds of earth ripped from the ground. We advance carefully, an eye on the murky water pooled in these shell craters.

The sun slowly makes its warmth felt through the grey air. The heat swells the forest and humidity rises in scrolls, as if the vegetation were being consumed from within. We make progress, but laboriously. Fallen trees block the trail. We snake our way between these felled mastodons, trying not to lose track of the path. I keep my eye on my watch. Nine thirty, eleven twenty, ten minutes before one.

You got a plane to catch? Olio kids me, slipping under a broken branch.

I act like I didn't hear. With a mocking eye, he watches me step up my pace. The sky has cleared completely. Beams of light break through the tattered foliage.

We come to a wide swath of toppled trees. At first, we have trouble understanding what we are seeing. A forest of fallen wood. An entire mountainside covered with broken trees. In one night, the storm swept away their patient upward progress. Nothing but a sea of uprooted trunks and split branches. Impossible to pick your way through that. We'll have to go around.

Olio tightens the strap of his bag. Like an acrobat, he scales the roadblock of broken limbs.

Come have a look, he calls from above, it's like dominos that fell on each other.

Against the afternoon light, he blends in flawlessly with the confusion of branches. It is two twenty.

Stop looking at the time and come on! he urges me.

We'd better go around this mess. Otherwise we might never find the trail again.

He replies, I can't hear his answer, then he disappears in the chaos. I clench my teeth, tie my sticks to the side of my pack, and climb onto the back of this monster made of smashed wood.

We climb, we hang on, we hoist ourselves, we go up, we slide down, we start all over again. I move slowly to spare my knee. If it gives way, I'll lose my balance and end up impaled on the broken branches. Meanwhile, Olio leaps agilely from one trunk to the next as if he knew ahead of time where to put his feet. I try not to lose sight of him, making my way through the puzzle of branches, bark, and needles. I have scratches on top of scratches, my pack gets caught, my hands are covered in pine resin. The crossing takes hours. I think only of where I am going to put my feet next, and like a log driver on a frozen river, I move carefully from trunk to trunk.

We finally reach the other side of the obstacle. I sit down on my pack to get my wits about me while Olio amuses himself by pointing out my scrapes and bruises and the torn hem of my pants.

We eat a can of vine leaves and look at the map. We're less than four kilometres from the valley where the Station is.

Olio puts away the map and stands up. He is ready to move on.

Look, I tell him, it's ten to eight, it's almost night. I'm aching all over. Let's sleep here in the open. Tomorrow at sunrise, we hit the trail. Okay?

5:20 A.M.

We get going as soon as dawn brings first light. We find the trail again that zigzags through the woods towards the Station. An hour later, we reach a wooden observation platform that overlooks the place.

The ski runs cut the summits above the valley into thin strips. The chairlift hangs in the air, empty and unmoving. At the top of the slopes, the burned remains of a ski shelter point skyward. Below, by the meandering river, stand the Station's three hotels with their balconies, windows, and antennae. A many-coloured sea of tarps and tents stretches out at their feet.

We squint to try and see what is going on down there. Tiny figures move from one place to the next, campfires smoke among the mosaic of makeshift tents, Jeeps are parked sideways across the access road.

We need binoculars, I say, trying to figure out where the guards might be.

A gunshot rings out in the valley below. The mountains send back fragments of its echo. Hunters stalking the woods.

Look, Olio calls, pointing to the yellow float plane in the river. The woman wasn't lying after all.

I give him a questioning look.

What about it? he justifies himself, you never know. Guess what I found in their bags.

I won't play his game, I'm tired of it.

Look, he crows, laying a bundle of banknotes on the edge

of the lookout. There was plenty more like this. Strange. Do you think it's still worth something?

No idea, I say, taken aback. Maybe you can play cards with it.

I don't really know what to think. Actually, I couldn't care less. We're at the Station. If we follow the trail that runs along the top of the ski runs, we'll pass the burned shelter, then meet up with the access road at the Park exit. From there, we will have just one day's walk.

You sure you don't want to go a little closer? Olio tries again, pointing at the hotel complex that obviously intrigues him. Just to get a better look?

I wave him off and start walking before he gets another crazy idea. We skirt the valley along the mountain ridges, then descend the far slope of the Park's mountains. The lower we go, the warmer and more humid the air. The vegetation becomes heavy and luxuriant. We disappear under a pergola of green. The rocky peaks of the Station are far behind us.

The day is dying when our trail meets up with the road. We hesitate, then take our chances. The gate has been knocked down and the welcome centre pillaged and squatted in several times over. In a wide, grey, gravel parking lot are any number of abandoned vehicles, including a school bus.

The place looks deserted.

We decide to camp in the bus for the night. We eat, then stretch out as best we can on the leatherette seats. I twist and turn in my sleeping bag in search of rest. I think of my family's camp. We're almost there. I can hardly believe it.

Olio shines the headlamp on the ceiling.

Actually, I liked school, he tells me. The bus would pick me up every morning at the corner. In class, my friends and I would laugh like fools, but we got the best grades. I haven't seen them since the blackout. I have no idea what happened to them.

8:05 A.M.

This morning, before we leave, Olio spends a long time staring at the stalled bus in the vacant lot. I take him gently by the shoulder and lead him forward, away from the past, and under the cover of trees.

Here and there, when the thick foliage opens, we can make out the fullness of the sky, the weight of the clouds, the heat where the sun breaks through. We follow a narrow stream through dense underbrush. Ivy and other vines wrap their way around the branches to drink in the daylight. We step over old, dead trunks, move through spots where the grass is taller than we are, and cross impossible thickets.

We walk past the obstacles without talking. Olio is ahead of me, but only by a few steps. He is not outdistancing me the way he usually does. He stops to sit down on a stump. He is crying. I drop my pack and sit at his side.

My brother got sick with the good weather. No one ever came. I took him on my back and we started out. After a few days in the forest, we still hadn't found anyone to help us. I had no more strength and my little brother was white from the fever. He died. He died in my arms.

I lean over and hold Olio tight. None of that was your fault, I whisper. I'm here now, I won't abandon you.

I was lost, he sniffles, very close to me, and I was alone. One evening I saw light. Three travellers around a campfire. I hesitated too long before going to see them, one of them fired his rifle in the air, he thought I was an animal. The others laughed. I hid until they fell asleep, then I stole their bag of supplies, and I swore I would leave the woods.

What was your little brother's name?

Olio, he murmurs, getting to his feet, his name was Olio.

I call to him and take off running, but my foot gets stuck under a root and I fall. Out of breath, I catch up to him on the bank of a river that makes a wide curve between two chains of mountains. The river flows powerfully, its depths reach far down. On the other side, I see the tops of the tall cedars towering over the rest of the forest.

This is it, I say, amazed, we're here. You'll see, we're going to be all right. I'm sure you'll get along with my aunts and uncles, especially Nep.

I kneel down at the river's edge and splash my face with cold water. I dig through my bag, change my shirt, and tighten my belt by a notch. Olio watches me, eyes hidden under his cap. Suddenly, I am nervous about being back with my family again. As if I wasn't sure whose arms I was throwing us into. I haven't seen them for so long. And I'm not alone.

With my family, I tell Olio, looking to the other shore, no nonsense and no stealing, get it?

He shrugs as if he doesn't know what I'm talking about. Then, with a smile on his lips, he asks me what time it is. I rub the trace my watch has left on my wrist and wonder where I could have put it. I look at the boy. He is holding it in his hand.

Let's go, it's time, he shouts, throwing my watch in the river, what are you waiting for?

Incredulous, I watch the flash of metal disappear in the current.

I glare at him. I feel like teaching him a lesson with the back of my hand, but catch myself in time.

What does it matter, we're finally here.

Light dances on the body of the river. I move to the very edge of the bank, take a deep breath, then whistle three times.

It is exclusive, pitiless. The forest is its law. The shadows its chessboard. Its reign descends from ancient times and it is proud of that. It refuses to admit that in these places nothing is taken for granted, nothing endures. Yet it is not the only one looking for light here. Every day, it labours, it hunts, it devours, and trades what it kills. Its members are noisy but skillful. To keep from killing one another, they stick together like a single body. And when they laugh, the earth trembles.

FAMILY

JUNE TWENTY-SEVENTH

I search the dark trees on the far riverbank. A light breeze lifts their branches and ripples shiver across the water's back. I wonder if they heard me. It is taking too long. I whistle again.
    I look for some other way to cross. Outside of swimming, I don't see how we could make it. Olio thinks that maybe there isn't anyone on the other side. I cut him short – my heart leaps, I spot a canoe farther down the river. The person is paddling slowly in our direction. Olio watches the canoe come near, still wary. When he is a few metres from the bank, I recognize the man. My uncle Herman. He has aged, his face has hollowed out and his hair is grey, but it's him all right. Even sitting at the rear of the canoe, he is as massive as ever. He comes up to the shore, braces himself against his paddle, looks at Olio with some curiosity, then turns to me with a smile.
    I'm filled with relief along with a bad case of nerves. I can't think of anything to say.
    What are you waiting for? Herman calls. Don't stand there like a couple of statues, get in.
    We scramble into the canoe. Herman pushes off. The others are not going to believe their eyes, he says. He points to my legs. I seem to have gotten over my accident. I nod, then look towards the tall cedars that rule the forest on the other side. Bent, leaning one against the other, they form a single mass that challenges the sky. The canoe moves

soundlessly. In front, Olio leans over the edge and stares into the river's depths where giant submerged tree trunks lurk like sleeping monsters.

We pass a bend bordered by a dense willow thicket. We hear the whisper of aquatic plants against the canoe's hull when we pull up to a wooden dock hidden between two rows of bushes.

Herman leads us down a path dotted with moss and crossed by roots. The forest is busy with birdsong. I move forward, holding my breath. For once Olio stays by my side.

We've got company! Herman shouts when we come into the clearing.

My shoulders relax as soon as I spot the lichen-covered roof, the triangular attic window, and the old porch. Framed by tall grass and camouflaged by climbing plants, the camp looks smaller than I remember.

The door opens and my aunt Hesta steps out. My heart kicks into high gear. I push my walking sticks into the earth, throw off my backpack, and go to her like a moth to flame.

You still have your mother's eyes, she tells me. Then she hugs me so tight I can hardly breathe.

My uncle Boccus comes out from behind her and grabs my hand in his vise grip. He has aged, too. His skin is deeply lined and his cheeks are covered with tiny red veins.

We figured you'd come looking for us, he exclaims, an eye on my boots. But we never thought you'd make the trip on foot!

Diane and Darès join us. They are wearing old camouflage clothes, and amazement stops them in their tracks. Diane embraces me, then hides her emotions behind a quick wave of her hand. Her eyes, set off by crow's feet, are as sharp as ever. Darès pulls me to him and slaps me on the back. He whispers into my ear that a mechanic like me should have been able to find a four-by-four in the village to fix up. We both laugh.

My aunts and uncles turn their attention to Olio. He stands close by me, afraid to make a move. I want him to step forward so I can introduce him to my family.

What are you doing with him? Where does he come from? Where are his parents?

He was alone in the forest, I say, as Olio shelters behind me.

Seeing his discomfort, Hesta steps in and leads us towards the house.

Come, you must be starving.

We climb the porch steps and go inside. The afternoon light slants in through the window. Olio freezes when he sees the impressive moose antlers hanging on the wall. My grandfather's trophy. I run my hand over the table in the centre of the room and feel the familiar marks worn into the wood. The Braille of the past. I can't remember the first time I came here. This place has always been part of my life. The gas range, the wood stove, the attic stairs, the rocking chair – nothing seems to have moved from its rightful spot.

My aunt puts a meat loaf in the oven and serves us glasses of water. I lift mine in front of the window and watch the tiny particles turning circles in the light.

The best water in the world, my grandfather used to say. It tastes like the mountain.

I quench my thirst and turn to the calendar on the wall. The month of June, last year. The picture shows a ruined temple with columns and stone gods on a mountaintop halfway between forest and sky. On the squares for the days, notes have been made, then crossed out, names encircled with arrows.

The door opens with a bang and two blond-haired children run into the room. Olio watches them warily. My cousin

Sylvia appears with her happy expression, sparkling green eyes, and wavy hair. I jump to my feet to greet her.

What a surprise! she says gaily. You haven't changed a bit.

I smile, knowing the years have not spared me. Sylvia's children run circles through the room several times, knock over a chair, then head out the door, slamming it behind them.

Those are my twins, Rémi and Roman, Sylvia tells Olio. You'll see, they raise a ruckus, but they're really very nice.

The wooden stairs creak. Someone is coming down from the attic. My cousin Janot. He was still a kid when I left the village a dozen years back. Today he is a man with long hair, a scraggly goatee, and loose limbs.

Do you see who's here? Hesta points. They made the whole trip on foot, can you believe it?

Janot greets us, sizing us up.

You came from the village?

Yes.

What's it like back there?

Let them eat in peace, Hesta interrupts him, taking the dish from the oven.

The smell fills the room and our mouths water. We wolf down our piping-hot portions as my family looks on in disbelief. The food is delicious. Olio chews noisily and I elbow him, though not hard. When I finish my plate, I look up. An attentive silence fills the room. I begin to talk.

Briefly, I describe the way I came, how I met Olio and crossed the Park. My aunts and uncles listen, eyes wide, then ask what shape their houses were in when I left.

They were looted, but they're still standing. The village was practically empty. Everyone ended up leaving.

My family looks dismayed. Darès states that they did the

right thing, seeking refuge here. He knew things would turn out badly back there.

Though I am satisfied to have finally reached the camp, I am not free of resentment. Olio was right. I have caught up with them because they left without me. Uncle Boccus senses my change of mood and leans over in my direction.

We didn't want to leave you on your own, and you know it. But we couldn't bring you with us. It wouldn't have made sense, what with your injuries and the long trip in winter. You couldn't even stand up, remember? But we left you in good hands. The proof is that you're here!

I look at my palms covered with blisters, my scratched-up forearms, my dusty clothes. Next to my family with their well-mended shirts and pants, their clean hair, trimmed nails, and brushed teeth, I realize just how dirty Olio and I are.

In any case, Hesta adds enthusiastically, we're happy to see you! I still can't get over it. Take your things up to the attic. And pay a visit to the shower, it'll do you good.

Enjoy! Darès tells me. The sun's been shining all day, you'll have hot water.

The two last words help me forget the rest.

The shower is a little structure made of wood trellis around the side of the building. A black tank was installed on the roof and the pressure is good. I soap myself up for a good long time. The water flows over my head, my neck, my chest, it covers me and rinses the dirt from my body. When it's Olio's turn, I shave using the little mirror hanging on a tree. My face is revealed, and my features surprise me. I don't have an ounce of fat. My skin is stretched tight over my ropey muscles. I try smiling at the mirror, but it tells me I'm a collection of nerves. When he comes out of the shower, Olio laughs at my smooth cheeks. We put on the clean clothes we were given and go to join the others. They have assembled in the clearing around a big heap of branches ready for burning. Their noisy camaraderie touches me.

This calls for a celebration! Boccus announces as he opens an unlabelled bottle.

Darès lights the fire. We move closer to one another and toast our reunion. My eyes tear up when I taste the sugary stuff.

It's mead, my uncle says, tipping the unmarked bottle in front of the light. It comes from the coast. Careful, it's stronger than it seems.

He's right. Drunkenness comes quickly, chatty and comforting. The conversations flow together. We talk about the blackout and life at the hunting camp and conjure up old memories. The echo of our voices carries far, as if the mountains were joining the party.

I take a minute to look around. Trees have been cut down to enlarge the clearing, two army tents serve as dormitories, the old shed has been replaced by a bigger and sturdier one with a heavy padlock on the door. To keep the bears out, I imagine.

You're not doing too bad here, I say to Darès as he puts skewers of meat on the coals.

Wait, you haven't seen anything yet. When we decided to move here last fall, we brought everything we needed. You know us. The two pickups and the van were filled to the gills. It took us a whole week to ferry everything here by canoe from the dock. But it was worth the trouble! he tells me. Like your grandfather used to say, we may be at the far end of the world, but at least we've got peace and quiet.

The flames climb towards the sky and compete with the evening light that slowly settles in. After the meal, Olio curls up at my side. I bet he sipped some of my mead.

Your mother would be happy to see us all together, Hesta tells me. And most of all she'd be happy to see you with the little guy. I like his looks. I can't help but smile when I see him wearing that green and yellow cap. Luperc had one just like it.

I picture Luperc's face, his stacks of wood, his trailer. I go and fetch the letter he entrusted to me and give it to my aunt.

You met him at the Park entrance, she says hurriedly, is that it? Is he all right? Getting along? The dogs still with him?

I tell her how he gave us shelter and supplies. He is living the best he can. My aunt thanks me and hides the letter in the pocket of her jacket.

When the dew begins to fall on our shoulders, we add more wood, and warm light envelops us. Boccus opens another bottle. Everyone is in fine form. The night is clear, and I don't feel my knee or my painful shoulders anymore.

Then, through the laughter and conversation, an enormous sense of exhaustion comes over me. I wish everyone good night, gather up Olio in my arms, and climb to the attic.

Tell me, he asks, half asleep, where's your uncle Nep?

JUNE TWENTY-EIGHTH

When I open my eyes, the sky is full of light. It comes into the attic through the triangle of the window and winds around the roof beams. A pile of old mattresses in a corner. It is warm, the sheet-metal roof makes clicking noises, and flies circle around my head. Olio's bed is empty. So is Janot's. Through the floorboards, I hear fragments of conversation, cups and dishes clinking together, the squeaking of the door. Reassuring noises.

I remember my watch carried off by the current and wonder what time it is. I get up and go downstairs. The steps creak beneath my feet. Boccus is sweeping the floor. Herman is doing the dishes. Everyone else has gone out.

My uncles chuckle when they see my morning-after look and point to the leftover oatmeal and coffee. I pour myself a cup and go out onto the porch. I savour every sip in the brilliant morning light. I can hardly believe it: plenty of food, mead, and coffee. My family really knows how to get along. I'm lucky to be here.

I take in the beauty of the tall bending cedars, the heap of wood in the middle of the clearing waiting to be split, the small smokehouse made of grey planks, the paths disappearing into the woods in all directions. Olio emerges from the trees and comes over, holding a stick.

Look, he says, I whittled down the end with a knife.

He turns around, takes one long stride, and throws his

javelin. It curves gracefully through the air and sticks upright in the ground between some stumps. The twins, who were watching him, applaud.

Olio goes off to retrieve his weapon as Hesta comes out to stand beside me.

How long does it take? she asks, her voice veiled with emotion.

To do what?

Cross the Park and get to the welcome centre.

My aunt is holding Luperc's letter. I picture the mountains we crossed, the obstacle of fallen trees, the chaos at the Station.

It took us over two weeks. I'm sorry. The access road is blocked, you have to go around the Station on the forest trails.

Hesta sighs. Her eyes are misty with tears. I grasp for something to say to change the subject. Olio goes by with his javelin. The twins follow at some distance, whispering to each other.

What about Nep? I say finally. Isn't he here?

My aunt's eyes bore deep into the ground.

Nep went away, she answers, looking for some way out of the question. You know, even though we had all we needed, the winter was hard. We were living on top of each other. It drove Nep crazy. I did my best to make him stay; he wouldn't listen. This spring, he left for the villages on the coast. Seems he has friends there.

I am more than a little surprised. Something happened to put that long, serious look on my aunt's face. She puts her hand on my shoulder, then goes inside. I finish my coffee as I tour the camp. I know Hesta isn't telling me everything.

Later, I come across Sylvia. Today is Sunday, she says, everyone can do what they want. My aunt Diane is cleaning and oiling her rifle and talking with Darès. Boccus is having a nap in the shade. My cousin Janot has his back against a tree, and he is absorbed in a book.

I had a talk with Olio this morning, Sylvia confides, lowering her voice. He told me how his parents died in a plane crash three years ago. Then the foster homes, the blackout, the iffy group of people he fell in with when he came to the region. And how you met. Did you know his father was a mechanic like you?

Yes, I say, feeling the effort not to say anything. He told me all that.

The twins come running and throw themselves into their mother's arms. She teases them lovingly, then asks if they want to go for a walk.

As I watch them disappear into the woods, the bushes rattle behind me. I wheel around. Olio is lurking in the foliage, javelin on his shoulder.

What are you doing there?

Nothing. I was playing. What about you?

JUNE TWENTY-EIGHTH

In the evening, we all gather around the ancient wooden table. The sky clouded over at the end of the afternoon and it's dark. Darès motions to Herman, who heads out the door. A few moments later, a motor starts up and yellowish light fills the room.
I look up. Amazing! A circuit of wires and bulbs is attached to the ceiling. Olio's eyes shine with delight.
I told you we had a few surprises for you, Darès says proudly. We've got a generator!
What about gas? I ask, astonished.
When we made up our minds to come here, we knew we wouldn't be returning any time soon. We took all the gas we could. We've got enough for another two years.
It all seems too good to be true.
My family laughs at our state of amazement. The meat loaf is served, and under the wavering light, the conversations rise over the sound of utensils. Olio is sitting next to me and we watch, fascinated by everything around us. The twins making a ruckus. Herman and Janot locked in debate. Diane describing the summer itineraries of moose.
After the meal, Darès takes down the calendar. The wood is paler where it hangs compared to the rest of the wall stained by time.
It's last year's edition, he tells me. But what difference does it make if the days have moved up a notch? The important thing is to have a way of keeping track. You know

us, we're not afraid of work and we know what we want. It wasn't always that way. So now, every Sunday evening, we divide up the week's chores. Everyone has to pitch in.

Boccus imitates his brother's self-important delivery. The family bursts out laughing. Darès ignores them and goes about handing out the jobs like a dispatcher. Diane and he will go hunting, Hesta will do the cooking, Herman will see to the snares, and the others will finish preparing the meat for the next trip to pick up supplies.

And this week, Sylvia adds, Janot will be Rémi and Roman's schoolteacher.

What do I do? Olio wonders, tipping the chair forward on its front legs.

Start by sitting up properly, Hesta tells him. Tomorrow you'll be with Janot and the twins.

Olio looks my way, choking back his protest.

You told me you missed being in school, I remind him.

Sylvia gently tells him not to worry, Janot is an excellent teacher. Then she gets up to put her children to bed.

And you, Darès says, pointing at me with his pencil, I hope you remember a few things from your trade, because you're going to have a look at what's wrong with the outboard. We're going to be needing it very soon.

Where are you going?

To my friend Marchand's place, Herman chimes in. It's farther down where the rivers meet. That's where we get our supplies.

What do you pay with? Olio asks, serious for once.

The whole family laughs.

What do you think? Meat!

The electric lightbulbs seem to have arrived from another world. Their intensity varies according to the generator's irregular output. As if the motor was having trouble keeping time. When Darès replaces the calendar on the wall, everyone gets up and leaves the table. I watch the way my aunts and uncles move. They throw back their shoulders, which makes them look like giants. I glance up at my grandfather's hunting trophy that dominates the room, and understand how they could have felt hemmed in last winter in this small space.

A small cloud of insects circles the lights, banging against the bulbs over and over again. When the low growl of the generator ceases and everything goes dark, I figure I'm the only one still up. Then I see a figure on the porch. Boccus having a cigarette. I join him. He offers me one, pointing out that they have become precious these days. I thank him. We watch the moon rising above the spruce. Nearby, the clearing holds back the power of the forest. The fragile miracle of an oasis.

My uncle's voice rises between two scrolls of smoke.

We're going to need meat. It's the new currency. That's how things work. For flour, potatoes, alcohol, cigarettes – all the rest. But you can't believe everything Darès says. The calendar is fine and all, but the only law that counts is seniority. And he's the oldest.

When I go back inside to bed, I pass the calendar hanging on the wall. Sunday, June 28. Tomorrow another week begins.

JUNE TWENTY-NINTH

I come down from the attic as soon as I hear people stirring below. Olio is there, eating a bowl of oatmeal. Darès and Diane are in the doorway, ready to head out, both dressed in khaki, with their rifles on their shoulders. Behind them, morning has laid its hand on the forest. Like clockwork, the rest of the family appears, they sit down to breakfast, grumble about this or that, then get busy. Uncle Herman takes a key hanging by the door and tells me to follow him.

When he opens the shed door, my nose is filled with the smell of dried blood and gasoline. A piece of meat is hanging in cheesecloth, and there are bags of salt and a number of Mason jars. The other side of the shed is reserved for tools: a brushcutter, three chainsaws, an old Rototiller, and a compressor. The generator sits in the middle, hooked up to an exhaust pipe. At the back, several dozen gas cans and propane tanks are meticulously stacked. An extraordinary display.

We're not amateurs, Herman says proudly, then points to the outboard motor lying half-open in a scattering of tools.

I've tried everything, he says. I don't get why it keeps missing.

I turn the hood to see what make it is. A classic model, ten horsepower, black with red stripes on the side.

You've got to make it run, my uncle tells me, pointing at the jars of preserved meat. I'm going to Marchand's soon. And I don't want to have to row home.

I'll see what I can do.

If you have time, he adds before going out to check the snares, the generator and the chainsaws need maintenance, too.

I lean over the workbench just as Boccus and Hesta come in to take the folding table, fresh meat, and a sack of salt.

I think your little guy is going to like it here, my aunt says happily. He's sitting quietly with Janot and the twins.

I nod, pleasantly surprised. Finally, I'm alone with the motor. I am so used to the work, I don't have to think about what I'm doing. I change the oil, clean the spark plug, lubricate everything that moves, check out the possibilities. The carburetor seems particularly dirty. I open the bowl, unscrew the jets, take out the filter. I soak the parts in a little gasoline and scour each one with an old toothbrush. I turn on the generator to feed the compressor. The two engines howl as one inside the narrow shed. The uproar does me good despite everything. Like a quick return to the time spent in my father's garage. I run compressed air over the parts, put them back in their proper spot, and close the cover. That should do.

My hands are black with oil. They remind me of my past life, long gone now, like the oil underground and the age of dinosaurs. With the blackout, I figured my trade would flicker out along with the refinery and service-station lights. That didn't happen. The old world is tenacious, and everywhere I go, I'm afraid there will always be engines to fix.

I leave those thoughts behind and turn to the generator. Same problem with the carburetor. I evaluate the chainsaws – ditto. I think about it. It's probably because of the gasoline that's gone bad from exposure to air. Despite the stabilizer they put in these cans, it's inevitable. For the time being, things still work, but in a few months this fine hoard of fuel will not be worth anything except to choke motors.

A figure comes into the doorway. Janot.

The twins crowd in behind him to peek at what I am doing.

We can't find Olio anywhere, my cousin reports. We were doing a spelling test. I wanted to see how he was doing, but he threw down his pencil and ran away.

I sigh and reassure him.

I'll go see. He can't be far.

I question the team busy around the folding table. They shrug. No one saw him. I think of my hard-headed young friend as I look at the pots of cubed meat and the strips that have been pulled from the smokehouse. I start back towards the shed and spot Herman and Olio coming from the woods with some hares.

He caught up to me on the path, my uncle explains.

Olio is wearing his mischievous look. He is quick to tell me that one of the hares was caught by just a foot, and it ran off when they arrived, but he stopped it cold as it was about to escape. With his javelin.

Come on, Herman tells me, dropping their harvest at my feet. You show him how to fix them.

I am only too happy to oblige. As Olio looks on openmouthed, I skin them by pulling on their fur. Then I break their necks and force my fingers into their chest cavity. When I smell the acrid scent of the viscera and see the blood pooling under my fingernails with the grease and oil, I feel like I have been here for millennia.

Darès and Diane return at the end of the day. They are empty-handed, but Darès gets excited and points at the portions of meat on the table. He turns to me to tell the story.

This moose came up close on my left. He made so little noise I practically fell out of my seat when I saw him. He stopped in one of the open spaces, a few steps from the marsh. I braced myself against the window ledge. Boom. And that's exactly where he fell.

A bit of luck, Diane teases him, exasperated by her brother's boastful nature.

We go back into the house. Hesta has made liver and fries. The smell of goose fat sharpens our appetites. Olio and the twins are especially delighted.

There was a little group of snow geese that landed in the river bend in the spring, Diane begins proudly. Usually they don't stop in the forest, they fly way above our range. But this time I got a good dozen of them.

We all eat heartily.

These are the last potatoes of the lot, my aunt says. The rest have gone to seed.

Maybe we could plant them, Sylvia suggests.

Oh, yeah, where? Darès asks ironically. In the clearing between the stumps? If you ask me, we're better off stocking up on meat for Marchand and getting what we need that way.

What's it like at Marchand's? Olio asks.

Herman explains. Marchand is a guy who took over an outfitter's lodge that used to cater to rich salmon fishermen. He lives there now with his dogs and his guards and barters with everyone in the area.

We're lucky, he adds. He's been a friend of mine for a long while. He gives us a good deal for the meat.

Talking about Marchand, Darès asks me, what was wrong with the outboard?

JULY THIRD

We'll need oil, flour, oats, potatoes, and fresh vegetables if there are any. And mead, coffee, and cigarettes. Jars, candles, batteries. Tampons, soap, mosquito repellant, and powdered milk.

Sitting at the end of the table, Herman scribbles down the order on a scrap of paper. Everyone watches him noting down each item as if it were a guarantee, a delivery.

It is still early. The forest is dark, but the river sparkles with light. My uncles and I hook the motor on the back of the canoe. We rev the motor a few minutes before putting it in the water to make sure it is running smoothly.

You see, they protest, our gas burns perfectly. We put all the stabilizer we needed in it. Who do you think we are?

We load the meat carefully into the narrow craft, jockeying for a spot on the little dock.

Marchand won't believe it when he sees what we're bringing him, Herman declares, sitting down in the canoe.

Don't forget my books, Janot reminds him.

Herman nods, checks that he has everything he needs, then waves. He'll be back in a few days, he promises. We untie the canoe and Darès helps him push off. Herman lights a cigarette and lets the boat drift slowly into the middle of the river before pulling the cord. The outboard coughs to life, Herman gives it gas, and disappears under the arch of willows in a thick cloud of white smoke.

I don't know anything about the outfitter where Marchand

set up shop. But I remember the rich salmon fishermen we would meet on the river with their guides. My grandfather always laughed at the way they worked their fly-fishing gear.

We linger a moment on the dock, watching the clear water rush past. Under the thin film of the current, I see the glow of green stones and picture the pools under the hem of the tree roots where the fish wait. I look to my aunts and uncles.

You must have caught a few salmon, didn't you? And without a licence!

We did get a few, Boccus admits. Young ones that spent the winter in the river. The run hasn't begun yet. That's not normal this time of year. Something must have happened at the fishway.

The sun rises above the line of trees and catches us in our lethargy. Diane and Darès whip on the troops. It's time to go back to work.

At day's end, we are back around the table again. Darès mentions how dry it has been lately.

The leaves are hanging low already. It's going to be a hot summer.

Hesta puts a plate of partridge confit and a jar of pickled vegetables on the table. She found a raspberry patch, she tells us, farther down the river bank.

We'd better get them before the bears do.

Darès guffaws. If he comes across one, that will be more potted meat for Marchand.

When the meal is over, we lean back in our chairs and lick our fingers. After Sylvia puts the twins to bed, a velvety silence settles over us. Digestion takes all our energy.

What do you say to some cards?

Everyone's face lights up. Without a word, they leave the table and return a few minutes later with coins and bills. Darès hands me twenty dollars and runs through the rules again. Boccus deals. The cards slide smoothly over the wooden table. Eyes brighten and exclamations ring out from the first game on. Olio watches the cards and money change hands.

I want to play, he declares, then retrieves his bundle of cash from the attic.

Everyone stares. I start to explain where the money comes from, but Olio cuts me off.

We might as well use it, right?

At cards, there are no teams, no friends, and no family, Darès chortles.

Olio joins the game and the hands are dealt. Hesta whispers advice in his ear. Darès wins the kitty a few times, and Boccus has to take out more money. The games move faster. Olio just misses winning. Hesta tells him not to force it. Then for a while, no one wins outright. Everyone curses their luck or blames the dealer. The coins and bills pile up in the centre of the table. Fingers are crossed. Darès doubles his bet. Some fold, others stay in. When it's time for everyone to show, Olio comes out on top. Darès slams the table. We all jump and decide the end has come, it's getting late. Olio gathers up his winnings as my family stares daggers at him.

Come on, tell us where all that cash you had in the attic came from?

From the Station, Olio blurts out.

I thought you went around the Station and stayed on the mountaintops, Hesta reminds him.

We spent a night in a Park shelter with people who had come from there, I say to make things clear.

And they gave you that bundle of bills? Darès challenges him.

Exactly, Olio replies.

Anyway, who cares? What did those people tell you?

Nothing good. One of them was wounded and they were escaping.

JULY SIXTH

It's Monday. Herman is not back yet. I hope he isn't having engine trouble.

It is Boccus's turn to play schoolteacher this week. With the help of an illustrated encyclopedia that must date back several years, he teaches the children the difference between cold-blooded and warm-blooded animals. So far, he has been able to keep Olio's attention. I am happy to see the boy with other children. He needs the companionship.

I have been assigned to firewood detail. The morning wears on, the heat beats down, the logs are dense and heavy. The axe keeps getting stuck in their woody flesh. Splitting the wood is a battle. I breathe hard when I see how much is left to be done. The sun is beginning to make me see double. My head spins when I realize that summer, as strong as it may be, is only an interlude between two winters.

The hunters return at noon.

Darès was right, Diane calls to me, it's too hot. If we killed something, the flies would be all over it in no time.

The early afternoon is an oven. The forest trembles in the still air, and little by little inertia takes over our weary bodies.

Let's go raspberry picking, Hesta proposes, trying to stir us into action. We can make pies.

The twins are happy at the prospect, but Diane and Darès hesitate. Hesta ends up convincing them and we set out with our containers along the narrow path to the river. The twins zigzag through the forest. Olio wants to ambush them;

he follows them, staying hidden. A light veil of pollen floats in the air. Under the canopy, we glimpse the sky only in those spots where fallen trees have left a space. There, the rays of the sun awaken the dormant saplings, sharpening their thirst for light and their spirit of competition.

Up ahead, Darès is telling Janot how to detect the presence of a dominant moose, pointing to the antler rubbings against the tree bark. Janot does his best to stay interested, but my uncle's theories about the habits of big game mean nothing to him.

My cousin walks alongside me. In the sunlight, tiny blond hairs glow on her face. The piercings in her ears remind me that today's world has nothing to do with the one we grew up in.

Remember when we used to run through the cornfields? she asks with a smile.

I nod, my eyes on her. We were not much older than the twins. We could disappear for hours in those long green passageways. We had no care for our parents who were looking for us or the sharp edges of the leaves that drew blood from our arms and legs.

She changes her tone. How do you like it here?

It's good to be among family, I say quickly, and feel like I'm part of the clan again, and be useful. I must admit, you're very well organized.

Whatever else, Sylvia answers, we've got peace and quiet here and the children are happy. Especially since we started teaching them. That gives them a framework, it reassures them. I wouldn't have thought that last winter, but it's true, we're getting by not too bad. I even have some projects.

A woodpecker hammers on a dead tree, and the echo carries through the open maw of the forest. Boccus, who was behind us, catches up, whistling. The twins and Olio burst from the woods, delighted when we reach the raspberry bushes. My aunt was right, there is plenty of fruit. We push our way into the plants. The berries are big, red, and plump. Sometimes they burst between our fingers, they are that ripe. We concentrate on the work at hand. In the afternoon heat, besides Rémi and Roman buzzing around their mother, all is quiet outside of the scrape of the thorns against our clothes and the breeze slipping between the treetops. Then Darès's voice rises above the branches.

One day, I was out hunting with Hesta. Must be fifteen years ago. It was raining and we hadn't seen or heard anything. We were in the same blind, my sister and me, and we were keeping our voices low. She told me she'd heard people say that you could attract moose by hooting like an owl. That from a distance, the male mixes up an owl's cry with the noise the female makes. When the rain finally stopped and the clouds lifted, I told her go ahead, try your business with the owl. She hooted and we kept our eyes peeled, leaning on the open window, ready to shoot. My sister shoved me with her elbow, she'd seen something moving behind the branches. I braced myself and took off the safety. And you'll never guess what I saw in my sight.

It's too much for Hesta. She starts giggling.

An owl! Darès exclaims.

Laughter breaks out, everyone has something to say, then the noise fades as we go back to our harvest. We change spots as our containers fill. I stand up and stretch. My fingers are stained red and my forearms covered in scratches. I look for the others, but they are kneeling in the bushes. I make out Olio in the bush. He senses I am looking at him, turns my way, then, with his usual mischievous expression, he comes to my side. I crouch down to his level as he stands there, very close, with a playful look. A sunbeam frees itself from the treetops, clings to a branch or two, and somersaults down to us. Gently, Olio moves his small dirty face and rubs his forehead against mine.

Thanks, he says softly, thanks for taking me with you.

I feel warm inside. I close my eyes and hold fast to this moment with all my strength. When we step back to look at one another, I feel he is finally letting me see the person hiding behind his small dark eyes.

A cry rings out. My family jumps out of the raspberry bushes, worried. It's Sylvia – Sylvia's voice.

We head in her direction. Dark arrows shoot out of the underbrush. The twins, running, followed by their mother, out of breath.

A bear? Darès asks hurriedly, is that it?

He swears. His rifle is back at the camp.

Leaning on her knees, Sylvia takes deep breaths. Rémi and Roman say nothing, their eyes wide, as if their lives hung on what their mother was going to say.

Yes, probably a bear, she says, once she has calmed down. I couldn't see very well, it was hiding in the raspberries. The twins weren't very far from there. I was scared. I screamed and it took off towards the river.

Hesta walks Sylvia and the kids back to the camp. Bears are usually peaceful creatures, she reminds them.

Darès wants me to go have a look with him farther on. Before I can react, Olio sprints off towards the river. We follow. I try not to lose sight of him, but he is outdistancing me with every step. My uncle is far behind. I come out onto a large plot of ferns. Nothing moving anywhere. Olio lost us. The late afternoon light is scattered by the green lace of the plants. I examine the ground in search of tracks. In the distance, the rumble of the river slowly gnawing away at its banks. Darès catches up to me, sweating and gasping, just as I spot small tracks that follow a pair of boots that are much bigger. I whistle and call Olio. No answer but the broken echo of my voice.

My uncle studies the footprints and tries to imagine their path through the forest. He turns, wiping his forehead.

It's impossible. There's nothing and nobody else in this sector. Who could it be?

Maybe someone walking, looking for a place to sleep, I suggest, thinking of the nights spent in deserted hideouts.

Darès has his doubts.

We'll see. In the meantime, let's go get our raspberries.

I shrug, then call Olio again, worried for him and irritated by his headstrong ways. Again, no answer. I turn and fall in behind my uncle. Back at the camp, I am relieved to see the boy has made it back.

What about your bear? Darès asks him.

I followed his tracks to the river, Olio replies with a quick look at me, but I couldn't catch him.

JULY SEVENTH

I have been chopping wood since morning. I raise the axe and let it drop without forcing it, the log splits, and I set up another one. I am like an assembly line. The sun is leaden, the air stagnant, beads of sweat blossom on my forehead. I try to maintain the rhythm, but the axe falls from my hands. I look around. Olio is with Boccus and the twins under the tall cedars. At the far end of the clearing, Diane is coming back from the blind. She takes the folding table from the shed and sets it up not far from me with everything she needs to make ammunition. She talks to me as she works.

Once, a few years back, I went to the blind before daylight. Halfway there, two moose were standing on the path. Their breath made clouds of steam in the cold air. It was rutting season and they were courting each other like nothing else mattered. I waited for them to get closer to one another, and cross, then I fired. That morning, she tells me proudly, I got two moose with a single shot.

I watch her pour in the powder, calibrate the bullets, arm the detonators, and oil the final product.

We can never have too much ammo. Her voice changes. I haven't seen fresh prints, scat, or nibbled branches for a while. I don't know where the game went. We're on our own here, but we can't be the only hunters around. The heat doesn't help, either.

I look around. Summer is devouring the forest and the landscape is shimmering as if it were about to evaporate.

Hard to believe that in a few months this place will be buried in snow.

What happened last winter? I ask carefully. Why did Nep leave?

Diane sighs. Her hands lie flat on the table as if they weighed a ton. Darès comes out of the woods and unloads his rifle. He walks past us and gives us a suspicious look, but says nothing and heads for the house.

You'll have to ask him, not me, my aunt says in a low voice. Everything about her is tense.

JULY SEVENTH

Late in the afternoon, the sputtering of an outboard motor cuts through the sounds of the forest. Our faces light up and we head for the dock. The twins push and shove and Sylvia has to step in and calm things down. We watch Herman approach. He manoeuvres to make a careful approach, the motor coughs, and the canoe slips quietly towards us. Everyone is glad to see his cargo.

Darès asks what took him so long. Herman turns red.

What do you want? he answers, a foot on the dock. Marchand needed a hand. I couldn't refuse, could I?

My aunts and uncles glance at each other, suspicious. Herman is radiant but exhausted, his mind at rest. We begin to unload the canoe. Flour, oil, sugar, mead, tobacco, coffee, onions, carrots, five sacks of potatoes, ten sacks of salt, and plenty of other things, too.

Well then, Darès launches in, satisfied at the pile of supplies we have moved into the house, what did Marchand have to say for himself this time?

Herman bites his lip. Good news and bad news.

Start with the bad.

Marchand said he heard there have been thefts lately. Groups moving through the sector. They come down from the Station, it seems.

I think of the boot prints we saw yesterday. My aunts and uncles look worried.

Our territory is enormous, Darès replies. Stop worrying about that. What's the good news?

The demand for meat on the coast is bigger than ever. Marchand was very generous again. I got everything on the list and even eggs, butter, and maple syrup! Having friends is useful, don't you think?

Boccus agrees. He opens a bottle of mead and serves everyone a drink. When we clink our glasses together in a hearty toast, beyond our walls, we feel the forest briefly dropping its hold on us.

One more thing, Herman says unhappily, we won't be eating much salmon this year. People blocked the fishway and the salmon are stuck at the foot of the falls. That's why we haven't seen any here. People are net fishing them, smoking them, and selling them for a good price. Marchand managed to get his hands on a few crates. He gave me one.

We figured something like that would happen, Diane and Darès say. That's why we're hunting.

We finish divvying up and putting away the spoils. Olio and the twins chase after the small grey moths attracted by the sacks of flour.

JULY ELEVENTH

Hesta and Janot helped me out with the wood. It is all split and it just needs cording. But the heat is oppressive and the week's work has our muscles aching.

I'm going to look for Olio. He's not with Boccus.

You know, I do what I can, my uncle tells me, putting away the old schoolbook, but he just won't sit still. He ran off an hour ago. Of course, the twins absolutely wanted to go with him.

I look up and spot them strolling along the edge of the forest. Seeing them together touches me, and I ask if they would like to go to the stream to fish for trout. All three of them are eager and they go searching for worms at the edge of the clearing. Olio turns over the earth with a shovel. The twins help out by breaking up the clumps by hand. We head out a half-hour later with our bait and three wooden fishing poles. Sylvia calls to us as we are about to go into the forest and joins us.

At the stream, the children head for the nearest pool to drop their lines. Olio helps the twins hook the worms and unhook the little trout.

Sylvia and I sit on a rock in the sun. We keep an eye on the young fishermen, lulled by the water murmuring between the stones.

They get along perfectly, she says.

I smile. Sylvia closes her eyes. The sunlight makes her face and neck glow. Discreetly, I let my eyes wander down to her graceful legs. The cicadas make the forest vibrate. They are so loud my head spins. Summer heat envelops us, wraps around us, and covers us over. For a moment, I feel we are alone in the world.

We should have brought cigarettes and a bottle of mead, Sylvia says dreamily.

We hear crying a minute later. We jump to our feet and go to where the kids are. They have moved quite a way upstream. One of the twins fell and his boots are full of water. He is complaining that he was pushed.

I was only trying to catch him, Olio claims, looking away.

We head back to the camp soon after.

Despite the incident, the kids are in a fine mood. They caught a good twenty trout. We clean them and set them aside. The light of day's end draws out the shadows of the great cedars. Soon it will be time to eat. As we wait, some of us sit on the porch steps to enjoy the cool air.

The sound of a distant explosion breaks our contemplation. It sounds like a clap of thunder, but the sky is completely blue. My aunts and uncles lift their heads and glance at each other.

It's from a lot lower down in the valley, they agree, frowning.

Are there people there? Olio asks.

I don't think so, Darès ventures. Herman would have seen them coming upriver, right?

I suppose, he says.

Twilight stalks us like wolves, the air is still, mosquitoes shorten our conversation. We go inside and the appetizing smell of breaded trout removes all doubt from our minds.

JULY TWELFTH

Sunday morning. Hesta decides to make pancakes for Olio and the twins. But she cries out when she opens the sack of flour. A cloud of little grey insects rises around her.

We've got moths, my aunt says, discouraged. Marchand's flour is crawling with larvae.

A moment of heavy silence. Then, without a word, resigned, we get to work to eliminate the pests before they contaminate the rest of our supplies. We empty the shelves. We clean the kitchen from top to bottom with vinegar. We go onto the porch to sort through the rice and oats and sift the flour. We try and save as much as we can. A whitish cloud moves across the clearing. Olio and the twins run back and forth through it, waving their arms. We burn everything that has been infested in the fire pit as our three little white ghosts play their game.

We saved most of it, Hesta declares after taking inventory. We reacted in time.

Everyone is relieved, knowing we avoided a slow-acting catastrophe.

Maybe we should go wash in the river, Sylvia suggests to get our minds off what happened.

Dusted with flour, Olio and the twins are ready for fun. My aunts agree, Boccus and Herman, too. Only Darès resists, but he ends up giving in.

My cousin leads us to the edge of a deep pool, a few hundred metres upstream from the dock. We lay our towels on the burning stones of the riverbank, undress down to our underwear, then go down the slope to the water. The light is sharp and the pale skin of our backs and legs stands out against our tanned necks and forearms. The water is cold. Everyone freezes when they put their feet in.

I watch the group. At first my family looks like giants, but their posture, their stooped shoulders, sagging bellies, and wiry black hair on their backs show them in a different light. The same is true for my aunt Diane's slender figure and Hesta's generous curves. I look down at the pink scars that snake around my knees. In this great land of trees and mountains and rivers, the fragile nature of our bodies is all too obvious.

Olio laughs at our hesitation. He is the first to throw himself into the river. The twins follow him and urge us on. The water is fine after all, it's just the contrast with the heat of the air. We feel invigorated. Boccus swims across the river, climbs onto a rock that overlooks it, assumes the ape position, and hollers, beating his breast. He jumps, gathers his limbs together, and splashes us when he hits the surface. Our laughter rings out in one voice from shore to shore. My aunt Hesta jumps when Herman carries her into the water. I dive beneath the surface and open my eyes. The sun reaches down to the silty depths and sketches out the dark borders of the snags. Above, a multitude of arms and legs beat against the current.

The hot afternoon air embraces me when I leave the river and climb onto the bank. Sylvia is sunbathing, her eyes in the crook of her elbow. The twins gallop through the shallow water, sending up droplets of light. Darès and Diane talk with their hands on their hips as Olio combs the river's edge in search of skipping stones.

I go and sit with Janot on an old trunk washed up in the shadows between the forest's appetite and the riverbed.

A few clouds knit together, then break up. I try and start a conversation. I never thought I would see us all swimming together, I say. He prefers his book.

Before, I go on, when it was hot like today, everyone would get together at Boccus's pool. Remember? Except for Nep, I don't remember my aunts and uncles ever setting foot in the water.

Imagine, he replies, finally agreeing to look at me, our grandfather never would have thought his descendants would end up living in the camp he built.

The fleeting memory of my grandfather returns, his worn face, his cedar smell, his tobacco pouch.

Look at them, Janot says darkly, turning his head towards the group. Look at them, we haven't even been here a year and it's like the world before is just an old memory. I think they like it that way. We have enough gas in the shed to fill up the vehicles we hid under the branches at the drop-off. Why don't we just go back to the village? I had a life before all this, I had plans and friends. And I never liked hunting. Last winter it was tolerable. I charged my tablet when the generator was on and played video games all night. Then the batteries wore out. Good thing that Herman is bringing me back books from Marchand's. Otherwise I'd never manage.

My cousin stares at me. His eyes are red. I want to encourage him, tell him we're better here than in the village, but Olio interrupts. He wants to show the frog he caught. The twins come running to take part in the observation. They marvel at the colourful patterns on its back. Olio places it on the ground and pushes it with the tip of his toe. The frog won't react. He pushes it again, gets impatient, picks up a stone in both hands, and raises it above his head.

What's wrong with you?

Olio stops when he sees I'm serious. I hold my expression until he lowers the stone and walks away. The twins wonder what's next, they are frightened and fascinated, then they start bothering the frog, too. Sylvia turned when she heard me raise my voice, and now she orders her kids to leave the poor animal in peace. A canoe appears in the bend of the river. Olio goes out onto a rock, better to see it. Sylvia takes the twins by the hand and retreats a few steps. My aunts and uncles form a group and thrust out their chests as they watch the canoe.

Four people on board. Two men, a woman and a girl Olio's age. Rifle barrels stick out over the edge of the craft. Darès steps forward, crossing his arms. His show of self-assurance is a poor match for his transparent, soaked underpants.

The woman in front waves to us and lifts her cap. The girl and Olio size each other up. It only lasts a moment. They paddle past us and move upstream, unperturbed, until we lose sight of them.

We look at each other as if we had seen the same ghost. Questions whirl through our minds. The landscape shimmers in the heat. Herman coughs and points out that his sources are reliable.

People are moving through the sector.

JULY EIGHTEENTH

We all woke up after a pretty much sleepless night because of the heat. Another heavy, sticky day in store. The usual smooth mechanics of our morning routine take some time getting going. Herman suggests we could set aside our tasks and stack some wood before the sun gets too hot.

We form a chain across the clearing and pass each other split logs. Even Olio and the twins join in. At the end of the line, Janot piles the wood quickly.

I can't believe we have to start thinking of next winter, he sighs.

Darès shoots him a hostile look.

You should be happy with what you have and stack the wood more carefully.

My cousin grits his teeth. Some of us chuckle, then go back to the repetitive movement, the texture of the bark, the humid summer heat. In the middle of the chain, Diane and Darès break the silence and mention the people who came by in a canoe a few days back. They must have come from the Station, like Marchand said, and they agree they were probably just passing through. Since then, no one has seen any sign of them. Olio is absorbed in his thoughts. In the distance, a few vultures draw circles in the sky.

We keep up the pace until the sun forces us to quit and head for the shadow of the tall cedars. Janot drags his feet. The family makes a few mocking remarks because his cords of wood are so unsteady. He waves his hand in our direction to let us know how little it matters to him. The sun follows its path, and slowly the green shadow of the trees changes consistency. The kids run and hide in the underbrush. The heat does not seem to affect them. Sylvia asks them what they are up to.

Olio taught us a new game, the twins answer in one voice. It's called lost children.

They rush off. We talk about the good weather that's still holding. The level of the river. The moose that lurk in the confines of the forest. Our words fade, flow together, and scatter in the deafening stridency of insects. Louder voices pull me from my reverie. Someone has suggested a game of cards.

Sylvia takes Rémi and Roman into the house for a nap. Olio leaves them to their fate and runs off to get his money. We gather around a big stump. Boccus deals the cards, Herman raises the pot, and the game begins. Though we are not as quick as usual, cards and money circulate at a good pace. Olio applies himself to the game and follows attentively. I catch him when he cranes his neck discreetly to peek at Diane's cards. I call him out and he jumps. Diane looks at him warily.

Eyes straight ahead, she warns him. You know how to play now.

Don't worry about me, he tells her with the delinquent's touch as he wins the first hand.

I hold back a smile. The hands begin again, the pace steps up. Banknotes are piling up on the stump. The sum is considerable. Our nerves quicken. Olio fidgets, then lays down his whole bundle of cash. We try to reason with him but he won't listen. A few of us fold. Darès and Boccus exchange a sly look and put down everything they have, too. Jaws are clenched.

The cards' turn to talk, Hesta tells them, show your hands.

Silence. They make their calculations. Darès prevails. He celebrates as he gathers up the pot.

I always win in the end, he claims, referring to the last game.

Olio gets up, furious. Diane urges him to calm down. He looks at us with his burning black eyes.

It's a game, Hesta reminds him, only a game.

I turn and offer him my hand.

Don't touch me, he orders, then heads into the woods.

All eyes are on me. Diane shakes her head. Boccus chuckles.

Say something! Darès urges me.

I tell them it's better to leave him alone. He needs time. The game resumes. Without much conviction, we win, we lose, we recover our money. Soon the heat gets the better of us and we decide the game is over. Enough is enough. Our damp hands stick to the cards, sweat drips in our eyes, we can scarcely wave away the flies that turn heavily around our heads.

Olio returns a few hours later as we are getting the meal ready. I am relieved he wasn't gone longer. Everyone eyes him and waits for an explanation. He looks like he has been running. We ask him what's happening.

I found a dead moose.

JULY EIGHTEENTH

Olio leads us down towards the river. We go along an open plain, like a savannah, between two valleys. The vegetation is dry and twigs snap underfoot. We don't even have to mention our fear of forest fires. The way is long and some of us start to complain. Olio ignores the protests until we reach the body of a young moose. Its eyes have been pecked out, its belly is swollen to the breaking point, and flies are buzzing all over it. Diane goes over to the inert mass worked over by the sun.

Look, she points with her foot, it was hit by a bullet in the shoulder, at the top, right here. Probably a few days ago. It came here to die, from the infection.

Shot by who?

Not by us, that's for sure, Diane says angrily. We never miss. And if we do, we track it down.

We stand in silence in front of the heap of wasted meat.

Stinks like hell, Hesta says, backing off.

We move away. Death will do its work with the impassive forest looking on. Questions and speculation on the way back. I half listen to their vain words.

People are hunting on our land, Darès concludes. We're going to have to look after the territory better. And keep our eyes open. That moose should have been ours.

At night, through the attic's small triangular window, Olio, Janot, and I listen to the call of coyotes feasting on a fresh carcass.

JULY TWENTY-SIXTH

Just before sunrise, the camp awakens. A few footsteps, sentences spoken in low tones, stifled laughter, the sound of boiling water. The last week went by like one day repeated seven times. We are a collection of acts during the day. A collection of words in the evening.

The heat wave burned itself out. Boccus and Herman joined the hunt to better our chances of getting a moose or spotting intruders on our land. For the time being, no one has seen an animal or an outsider. Diane says the forest is strangely quiet. Still, she killed three wild turkeys. They crossed right in front of her, gobbling away, as she was going to the blind. She had three bullets in the charger. And Hesta brought back a dozen hare from her snares.

The game is more than enough to feed us. And even keep some for later. But it is far from enough to trade with Marchand, at least that's what my family says.

Earlier in the week, Janot's cords of wood collapsed. He had to begin all over again, and he was criticized for not caring enough. He worked obstinately, eyes on the ground, lips tight, until night stopped him.

Today is our day off. A good time to run the riverside washing machine. Olio comes with me. We sit on the bank and punish our dirty clothes in the water bubbling around the stones. Then we stretch everything out to dry on the pebbles along the shore. A contrast between the colours of the cloth and the overwhelming green of nature. The sun heats my back. The river whispers close by. Olio gazes at the mountains of the Park that rise above the forest. I think about the blackout, the Station, the village where I spent the winter, the mystery of the coast, and tell myself how strange it is not to know what is happening beyond what I can see with my own eyes. Having so little news of the outside world. And nothing but meat and the seasons to help us look into the future.

We join the others for the meal. Sylvia tries to feed the kids, but they won't sit still. Darès picks up the calendar, and despite the twins' racket, he starts assigning jobs for the coming week. Boccus and Herman mock their brother's ceremonious delivery, and Hesta interrupts the procedure and asks Diane and Sylvia if they want to run out to the lake with the twins. The three women consult each other silently as Darès stands there, holding on to the arms of his chair. Particles slowly vibrate in the air. I turn to Boccus.

What lake?

Last fall, he explains, they opened up a path that leads to a lake a few hours away. They built a shelter with tree trunks and tarps. And put together a little aluminum rowboat. They go out there from time to time. To bring back fish, of course, but for a change of scenery, too.

If we can't have moose, Hesta points out, at least we'll have trout. Diane and Sylvia back her up, and the three of them stand, start packing their bags, and head for the lake, taking the twins with them. Janot and Olio watch them disappear into the arms of the trees.

Darès hangs the calendar on the wall without noting down a single item. He turns to the two boys staring at the forest.

It's not too late, he teases them, you can still catch up with them if you don't want to stay with us.

Herman laughs. Boccus rummages through the supplies in the kitchen. He looks up and smiles at his brothers.

Our sisters left with three bottles of mead. But we still have two cases left.

It's like a new day has begun. We sit out on the porch to enjoy the afternoon light. The warmth of the mead dissolves our uncertainties, our trapezoids ease up, and for a moment time loses its hold on our lives.

I watch Olio scuffing across the clearing. He is blowing on a pinwheel. He must have found it among the twins' things. I look across at the army tents my family uses as its dormitory.

You don't mind sleeping in the attic? Boccus asks me.

It's not so bad.

That's because you weren't here this winter, he grumbles, we were sleeping all together up there like sardines.

All of you snoring like diesels, Janot tells them.

Maybe, Darès admits, but at least we were warm.

Olio comes back after a while, looking preoccupied.

Is it true the villages on the coast are hooked up to wind turbines?

The question takes everyone aback. Including me. I thought he had stopped being interested in the coast.

With the variations in tension before the current went down, Darès argues, the transformers burned out. And you can't fix them just like that. The turbines can turn all they want, that doesn't mean the network is in any kind of shape.

Life must have gone back to normal somewhere, Janot objects, electricity or not.

Oh yeah, really? Darès challenges him. What do you know about it?

If that wasn't the case, Nep would have come back, my cousin mutters, shrugging his shoulders.

A thorny silence darkens the afternoon.

I don't know what's happening anywhere else, my uncle thunders, finishing off his glass in a single gulp, but I do know Nep is never going to set foot here again.

Boccus and Herman carefully avoid the conversation. Janot is restless. Darès stares him down. His aquiline features cast shadows over the plane of his face. He rises slowly, gets his rifle, and walks into the clearing.

Come with me, he orders his cousin once he has set up a line of empty bottles on one of the cords of wood.

Janot hesitates. His skin is pale, practically translucent.

It's okay, he stammers, it's really not necessary.

When you live in the woods, Darès insists, you have to know how to shoot. You can't just count on other people, right?

Janot breathes out heavily, climbs down from the porch, and accepts the rifle. He takes his time getting into position.

Relax, Darès laughs at him, it's not going to blow up in your face.

Janot concentrates. We hold our breath. Olio claps both hands over his ears. Janot fires and misses. My uncles make the usual remarks as he reloads and aims again. This time, when the detonation burns our ears, one of the bottles has been blown to pieces.

Is that the one you were aiming at? Boccus mocks him, holding his stomach.

My cousin makes a face and rubs his collarbone. Relieved, he quickly refills his glass.

You see, you're getting there, Darès claims. Pretty soon you'll be joining the hunt.

Janot avoids his eyes. My uncle turns my way and lifts his chin.

Go ahead, show us what you can do.

I haven't fired a gun in the longest time. I had forgotten how heavy this kind of weapon is. I shoulder the rifle. I close one eye and train the crosshairs of the sight on the middle bottle. I breathe out slowly and between two heartbeats, I squeeze the trigger.

Click.

Nothing happens. Mocking laughter erupts behind me. I curse. Janot's bullet was still in the chamber.

You want me to try? a small voice asks.

Leave me alone.

Come on, please.

I told you to leave me alone.

I get back in position, aim, and fire. The recoil shakes my entire body, my ears ring, and shards of glass go flying. Glowing, I look back at my uncles.

You haven't lost your touch, Darès congratulates me, raising his glass. Whose turn is it now?

Herman and Boccus line up next to Darès, ready to accept the challenge. The three brothers take turns, the shots follow non-stop, the bottles burst into pieces like peals of laughter.

Diane couldn't have done better! they say proudly.

Boccus tells the story of one autumn when their sister practically gave them a heart attack. It was a rainy morning. They had all gone to bed late the night before and she was the only one with the strength to get up. When the shot rang out inside the house, they nearly went through the ceiling. They stared at each other and rubbed their eyes. Diane was standing in the middle of the room, rifle on her shoulder. They couldn't believe it. She had fired through the window. And she got the moose that was disappearing under the tall cedars.

A few more hunting stories follow. I have heard them all several times, but I listen to them with the same fascination as Olio. The time they dragged Herman's moose out of a swamp where it had fallen. The time the river was so high they could hardly tie up at the dock. The time Boccus's rifle jammed and an old male stood in front of him for an hour.

Twilight slowly settles over the clearing. This evening, no one is going to make supper. We'll go on drinking and snack on whatever is on hand. Darès lights a fire by throwing old oil on it. The flames leap towards the sky and are mirrored in our glowing eyes.

Seriously, Herman says, looking at the burning wood, I wish summer would never end.

No kidding, Janot answers ironically after knocking back his glass, as if anyone here was in a hurry to march back into confinement.

It could be worse, Darès lectures him. Never forget that.

The conversation hangs for a moment, then picks up again with jokes and reassuring, reheated stories. Boccus offers everyone a cigarette.

When's the next trip to Marchand's? he asks, carefully stowing his pack in his shirt pocket.

Soon, I hope, Herman says dreamily, serving himself more mead.

Boccus questions him silently.

When we have more meat, he answers, then launches into a goose-hunting story that dates back several years.

They were positioned at the edge of a field, hoping a flock would land by their decoys. Nothing doing. Towards the end of the day, Nep couldn't stand it anymore, he was sick of waiting. When a cloud of starlings settled in noisily in the tree above his head, he emptied his weapon into the air, yelling his head off.

Old Nep, Boccus chuckled, the man who talked to the birds!

Once Herman finishes laughing with the others, his face grows dark. He looks like a toppled colossus on his log. Shadows dance on his hunting outfit and cling to his broad frame. Boccus goes to his brother and puts his hand on his shoulder. They must be thinking of Nep.

Olio pokes at the fire with a stick. Embers rise into the sky as if they want to join the stars and shine the way they do, with the certainty that other worlds exist.

I take a deep breath and turn to Darès, determined to find out more. Before I can ask the question, Olio speaks up and takes the words out of my mouth.

What happened with Nep?

Darès stares down Olio and asks him what business it is of his. An uncomfortable silence crackles above the flames.

Nep is gone, he says impatiently. If he comes back, we'll welcome him. We're still his family as far as I know. In the meantime, he can't do anything for us and we can't do anything for him.

You say that now, but you're the one who kicked him out, Boccus accuses him, his face flushed from alcohol.

Darès breathes out. He clenches his fists.

I wasn't the only one who was outraged by what Nep did, and you know it.

What did he do? I ask.

My uncle's eyes retreat deeper into his sockets and the lines across his forehead grow severe. Behind him, quiet firelight warms the sky.

Whatever he wanted to, he answers, turning the drink in his glass.

It wasn't just that, Herman adds. Nep wanted to leave. That's what he told me when I took him to Marchand's so he could go up to the coast. He couldn't take it anymore. The middle of the woods, winter, the blackout, the calendar, us.

Relieved when we drop the subject, Herman picks up a piece of bark and rolls it into a tube. He puts his mouth to it and imitates the longing call of a female moose. The cry fades into the night.

You need to put more emotion into it, Boccus says, and takes the instrument from him.

We laugh at his attempts. Darès tells him he should try the dominant male, but his grunting doesn't convince us.

The tension drops as quickly as it had risen. We open another bottle. It goes from hand to hand as my uncles retrieve more stories, their eyes sparkling with mead.

What we need is a moose like Pa's trophy in the big room! Darès declares out of nowhere.

The bull that knocked down trees like a storm! the brothers cry out together.

But their togetherness lasts only an instant, because they can't agree on who has the true version of the story. The words pile up in a disorderly heap. I'm drunk. The night drags on and my uncles seem to be speaking a foreign language.

The bark tube ends up in Olio's hands. He imitates a young male with astonishing accuracy. We all turn in his direction. He tells us he should be the one to go hunting. My uncles burst out laughing, figuring the first shot would knock him on his butt. His head down, Olio steals away to bed.

I like your little guy, Boccus tells me, his breath warm and ashy. He comes from another planet.

I glance at the dark house. Dwarfed by the forest, crushed by the starry sky, it doesn't look like much. I hiccup as I try and evaluate the angle of a giant cedar that seems ready to fall on it. Everyone agrees the tree has always been that way. Tall cedars all tilt a little, but they hold each other up.

In the wavering firelight, my uncles look the same. A few embers escape and shine as long as they can before fading into darkness. On his own, Janot looks up at the stars, weary of our conversation. I sit down next to him and ask what he is thinking about.

The pickups we hid under the branches on the other side. Nep was right. Staying here is crazier than going elsewhere. Everything can't have stopped everywhere.

I nod, but don't know what I'm agreeing with. I lean on my elbows. Soon it is my turn to surrender to the vertigo of the heavens.

The thicket of my uncles' voices slowly settles, as if they were sinking into a swamp. Everything is quiet but for the low rumble of the coals.

I see one! Janot exclaims in the quiet that seems surreal.

One what? they ask.

A satellite. Look, it's going to go right past the top of that tree, over there.

We spot the little white dot calmly following its trajectory through space.

Do you think it's still working?

A question with no answers. Then, in an order I can't fathom, the night swallows us up, one by one.

JULY TWENTY-SEVENTH

When I awake the next morning, my eyes have sunk into their sockets. I eat something, take some headache pills I find in a drawer, then go out for fresh air.

The morning is no longer young, and the light is blinding. The screeching insects, the singing birds, the hammering woodpeckers – the noise makes my head spin. In the clearing, empty bottles shine by the fire pit and a plume of smoke rises from the ashes. Olio is happy to see me on my feet, but his enthusiasm cools when he realizes how amorphous I am. He wheels around and disappears into the tall grass. Then returns with a few insects and throws them into a spider web under the porch. He stands there and enjoys the show.

I interrupt his observations and try to redeem myself by promising to go hunting with him soon.

Really? he says, his eyes shining.

For real, I say, then run my hand through his hair. My uncles get up, one after the other, dry-mouthed, the folds of their pillows printed on their faces. Maybe it's fatigue, or his headache, or our conversation last night, but Darès is more irritable than usual. He hands out our jobs for the week, his head bent over the calendar and his cup of coffee. We get moving, no questions asked, like fouled-up old machines lurching into action with a cough and a sputter.

I have been given the mission of ripping off the wild vines climbing up the back of the building. They are solidly fastened to the wooden planks. I yank on them, using my weight to pull them away. At one corner, a worm-eaten plank comes loose, caught in the vines' grasp. Ants hurry away under the rotten wood. They were happy there, gnawing away at the base of the building, emptying it of its substance and accelerating its deterioration without us any the wiser. I contemplate the panicked insects fleeing every which way, then feel their jaws digging into the skin of my ankles.

I go see Darès who is patching his hunting jacket on the porch. I inform him of my discovery. He shrugs.

There must some of that poison spray left over in the shed, he tells me, a sewing needle between his teeth. Use whatever's left, that'll do for a while.

Olio shows up just as I am about to apply the poison.

I want to do it, he insists, curious as the industrious little bugs run for their lives, then curl up and die in the chemical attack.

JULY THIRTY-FIRST

Darès informed Janot that he would have to learn to hunt like everybody else. And that tomorrow would be his first day. In the night, I heard my cousin turning over restlessly in his bed. Like it or not, this morning at dawn he set out with Darès, rifle on his shoulder.

Olio is disappointed that he wasn't invited. I repeat my promise.

Soon we'll go hunting. But in the meantime, do me a favour and go open the shed. We're going to try and fix the brushcutter.

I try and interest him in mechanical things, but the boy is bored. He rummages among the tools, gasoline, and meat.

Diane, Hesta, Sylvia, and the twins return from the lake at midday. Olio runs out to see them and helps them lay out their catch on the folding table.

Everyone is happy about the quantity and size of the trout.

Even if we'd wanted to keep fishing, my aunts and my cousin tell us proudly, we couldn't have carried any more.

Diane cuts the catch into perfectly triangular fillets, then tells us to salt them well and lay out the pieces crosswise in a wide wicker basket. Whirling around like mosquitoes in spring, Olio and the twins grab the fish heads we will use to make broth, and they set them to talking like puppets.

By the time we finish, the day is nearly done.

Tomorrow, my aunt continues as we put the basket in the

shed, away from the reach of animals, we'll turn the fillets over, and in two days we'll stretch them out on grills in the sun. Until we get a moose, at least we'll have dried fish.

My hands are viscous. I haven't taken a shower in several days. I head for the little wooden structure behind the house. I hear running water; someone is in there, I can make out a shape between the cracks in the boards. I am about to retreat when the shower door opens and Sylvia steps out in a towel.

I'm finished. It's all yours.

I want to move, but I'm frozen to the spot. Her wavy hair. Her shoulders. The curve of her hips. She picks up her clothes from the ground and smiles. Her movements are light and confident. Her body, foreign territory. Off limits. The moment lasts a few seconds, a minute, the whole summer, I don't know. We go past one another, our bodies touch, then Sylvia moves towards the house.

I get under the shower and soap up vigorously. The smell of fish is tenacious. Soon there won't be any hot water in the tank. I stay on despite the freezing stream, my breath short and my muscles tense, until my body is completely numbed.

Darès is back at day's end. We ask him why Janot isn't with him.

He wanted to spend the night in the blind. The moon is full, you never know.

Diane points out that you don't leave someone with no experience to hunt at night. Especially not Janot. What if he actually shoots something?

It'll be his initiation, Darès mutters, then goes to start the generator.

In the evening, Boccus serves us excellent trout fillets with rice and turnip purée. Everyone is delighted. We finish our plates in no time. After dinner, Darès plans our future jobs. Sweep the chimney, clean the engines, repair the outhouses.

Diane nods, but points out that we will have to hunt if we want any moose.

What will happen if we don't kill any? Sylvia wonders.

Impossible, Darès and Diane tell her in one voice. There have always been moose in the forest.

My cousin casts them a sideways look.

We could use a garden, she says. I brought some seeds with me. And Marchand must have some, too. We could plant beans, radishes, white turnips, even if it's late in the season. And we'd be getting the ground ready for next spring.

No one reacts. Hesta is the only one who seems to know about the project. She nods her approval. The others are afraid of all the work it would represent. I picture the luxuriant garden kept by the two sisters we met on our way towards the Park.

We even have a Rototiller! Sylvia adds, looking my way. We just have to fix it.

Not worth the trouble, Darès decrees. Think about it. The stumps, the rocks, the rodents, the insects. In the woods, hunting is the only thing that pays.

That doesn't seem to be true this summer, Sylvia says drily.

You never know. Darès tries to avoid the issue. Maybe Janot will get lucky tonight.

We're going to be here a while, Hesta interrupts them, hoping to end the debate, all options are on the table. You can sleep on it tonight.

The night breeze picks up, the generator falls silent, the camp settles down, and I hear someone snoring. Even Olio is sleeping deeply. I stretch out on my mattress, but my body turns away from sleep. Exasperated, I get up and go out for air.

I walk through the darkness, making no noise. Outside, I move across the wet grass of the clearing and piss in the light of the moon crowned by scattered clouds. Someone coughs behind me. *I am here.* I'm startled; I wheel around like a frightened animal and see a red glow in the night. Sylvia smoking, leaning against a stack of wood.

I go to her side and sit down. She takes out a cigarette and holds up her lighter.

You know, she tells me, you and Olio make a great pair. Maybe you can't feel it, but you being here really lightens things up.

I don't exactly believe her. She passes me the bottle of mead she was holding between her thighs.

Whatever our aunts and uncles say, we're stuck in this place. Family is a delicate balancing act. I'm happy you're here.

The moon pours its pale fire on the forest's edge. Singing insects put their imprint on the warm night. Sylvia moves closer with magnetic slowness. The black of her pupils is endlessly deep. Current moves through my belly. My body is pulled to hers. Our eyes hesitate, then our arms come together, our mouths are as one and suddenly we are slipping into an enchanting and terrible dream. We throw off our clothes, moonlight streams down on our shivering bodies, the dew on the grass evaporates, and moving fog surrounds us as if nothing else in the world was real.

As desire takes over, a gunshot rings out in the night. We freeze and look at one another. It comes from lower down the mountain. Too far away to be Janot. Then we turn the shot into the fruit of our imagination, and return to the intimate carnage of our flesh.

AUGUST FIRST

I wake up with a start as if fighting my way out of sleep apnea. Olio is already on his feet. My eyes travel across the attic, following the lines and breaks and knots in the planks. I feel my heart beating with disturbing precision. I close my eyes tight, then snap them open. Last night was not a dream. Nor a nightmare.

The stairs creak under my weight. Olio is alone downstairs. When he hears me, he looks up, greets me, then immediately slips out the door. I think he is up to something.

There is no more coffee. I look everywhere. Fresh out. We have gone through everything that Herman brought back from Marchand's. I settle for tea and go over to the calendar. Someone has turned the page. I look at the thirty-one white squares of the month of August. They are lined up beneath the photo of a coastal village, bordered on one side by a bottomless blue sea, and on the other, hilltops bristling with wind turbines.

I join Darès and Diane who are talking with Janot and Sylvia. It seems my cousin heard a gunshot last night. I look her way. She winks discreetly. Dewdrops shine in the morning light. Behind the foliage, bird, rodents, and insects are busy and the woods are brimming with secret lives. The smell of smoke catches our attention. The dry weather has us worried, and we try to figure out where the smoke is coming from.

Here! Sylvia points to Olio who is showing the twins

how to make a fire with a magnifying glass and sunlight. She removes the glass from his hands.

It hasn't rained for weeks. You could set the whole forest on fire, she scolds him.

I am afraid of his reaction. But with my cousin, he lowers his head obediently.

The day gets going. Sylvia is still set on her project to start a garden. Paying no mind to what the others think, she takes out the brushcutter to open up a space at the end of the clearing. The grass is tall and tough. It grows in a tangle to shoulder level. She keeps getting bogged down with the machine. But that doesn't stop her, she pushes on among the panicked insects, the plants bursting with sap, and the smell of burning oil.

I go into the shed to see if I can't get the Rototiller to work again. It's an old contraption. I wonder if it ever worked in the first place, and I'm surprised my family brought it here. But Sylvia can be persuasive. The gaskets have dried out and oil is leaking everywhere. I start to undo the hoses when I hear the children fighting. I stick my head outside and can't believe what I'm seeing. They are standing in a circle. One after the other, they slap each other, take the blow, choke back their tears, and start all over again, this time with insults. Incredulous, I yell at them and grab Olio by the arm. To my surprise, the twins leap to his defence and tell me it's their new game. A game to toughen them up. I order them to go see their mother and take Olio aside. He fights me, it's not fair.

What's wrong with you? I say, beside myself. They're kids!

I'm a kid, too, he replies, looking me in the eye fearlessly.

I raise my voice and tell him to go say he is sorry. He laughs. I try to reason with him. He laughs some more and asks if I want to play his game. I stare him down and he tries to hit me. I lose patience and shout at him to go upstairs to the attic. He gives me his sneaky look then gives in, happy to turn his back on me as I stand there uselessly, in a rage in the middle of the clearing. Hesta comes to my side. She witnessed the scene.

Diane is going to go see what's happening with Janot, she mentions. You should go with her; it'll do you good.

A minute later, I am following my aunt Diane towards the blind by the swamp. Her pace is brisk and determined. Her hunting clothes blend into the background, turning her into a furtive shadow.

Darès should have never left Janot on his own for a whole night, she sighs.

When the little grey wooden structure comes into view, we notice that the door is half-open. I climb up to have a look. The old car seats in front of the shooting window are empty. No sign of Janot except for some crumbs on the dirty floor. We comb the area around the swamp in search of moose tracks, blood stains, or bent leaves. Nothing. Just muddy water silently digesting the feet of the trees.

Normally it's one of our best hunting spots, Diane says.

She calls my cousin's name several times. Her voice trails off into the forest with the sound of singing birds.

Is Sylvia sure she heard a gunshot? she asks.

I think so, I answer, picturing us half-naked, our heads raised in the darkness.

We spot Janot's boot prints around the blind, but they soon get mixed up with ours, and others left by Darès and our group.

He can't be too far, my aunt mutters, picking up the path from the way we came.

Halfway between the swamp and the camp, at a spot where we have to jump over a stream, a cracking sound stops us in our tracks. Movement in the dead leaves. Probably a bear. Quickly and skillfully, Diane takes hold of the rifle she is wearing across her chest. The bushes along the path are particularly dense, and with the sun reflecting off the silver bark of the branches, we can't see anything.

It's coming closer.

Diane shoulders her weapon. I back off a step or two. The bushes shake a few metres away and Janot steps out of the forest's embrace with a stunned expression, covered in scratches.

I knew I heard something over this way, he says to save face.

What are you doing here? my aunt says, surprised.

You have any water? Janot asks, pulling thistles off his clothes.

My aunt points to the stream at our feet. When Janot bends over to drink, the barrel of his rifle aims straight at us. Diane pushes us quickly out of the line of fire, then takes his weapon and unloads it immediately. Janot laughs, embarrassed, then slakes his thirst in the little stream.

Diane counts the bullets in the charger and turns to Janot.

Did you fire this gun last night?

Janot straightens up. Water runs down his skimpy goatee. He shakes his head.

I don't believe you, my aunt roars at him.

Let's just go back to the camp, he pleads, his face falling.

We head back with no further discussion, watching how nature in all its disorder is reclaiming the path. When we reach the clearing, the twins run off to spread the news. Darès steps out onto the porch.

Where's that moose of yours?

There is no moose, Diane answers, but he's the one who fired.

In no time, everyone gathers around Janot.

I followed the river upstream, he admits, his features

drawn and pale. I wanted to get to the drop-off point to see if the vehicles were still there.

You were supposed to use the full moon to hunt, Darès reminds him, not go for a walk.

Janot rubs the back of his neck with a pained expression.

What kind of shape are they in? Herman asks.

I don't know, I couldn't see, there were people there.

Our eyes widen. The rest of his story promises no good.

They were sitting around a fire. One of them was even playing the harmonica. I wanted to get as close as I could without making any noise, but I tripped over a log. The music stopped and some of them started coming towards me. I ran up the slope of the mountain as fast as I could. They yelled something at me but I didn't hear it.

Were they armed?

How could I tell? It was dark.

How many were they?

I have no idea. I told you, it was dark.

And the gunshot? Diane insists.

It was nothing. On the mountain, I got lost. I decided to wait for morning, hidden up against a rock face. I kept the rifle in my hands, just in case. It fired unexpectedly. The safety must have come off as I was running. You should have seen the flame that came out of the barrel.

You should have seen the flame that came out of the barrel, Darès imitates him in a puny voice.

My uncle turns to us, and we all wonder who those people were and what they were doing. We are deeply worried and it shows.

We should go see, Olio speaks up.

All eyes turn in his direction. Quickly we agree to paddle the canoe up to the drop-off point. Olio is overjoyed.

You're not going anywhere, I tell him, taking him to one side. You can think about what you did this morning.

He raises his head and tries to stare me down. Then he spits on the ground and walks away, scuffing at the grass in the clearing.

And don't think I'm going to take you hunting anytime soon, I call after him, angered by his attitude.

AUGUST FIRST

We attach the motor to the back of the canoe, slip on our life jackets, and grab the rifles. Herman steers, Darès and Diane sit on the bench in the middle, and I am in front, looking out for snags and ready to help out with a paddle if necessary.

We travel against the current. The motor coughs from time to time like a pugnacious old bargeman. Darès and Diane watch over the banks, rifles at the ready. So far, nothing. The landscape moves through us. Trees bend low over the mirror of the river, the hull of the canoe breaks the water into shards, and trout take flight like dark arrows against the rocky bottom.

We come to a small set of rapids. Herman gives it gas and steers the nose of the canoe straight into the whirlpool. As I listen to the outboard sputter, I think of the gasoline supplies in the shed that are going bad a little more each day. I drag my hand in the cold water and watch its wake disappear. The logic of time is unstoppable and our lives are hanging by the thinnest of threads.

Herman raises his voice above the motor's racket and kindly requests me to watch out for snags like he asked me to. He has rarely seen the river so low, and that complicates his job. Rocks that are normally submerged have stuck their heads up. He starts telling the story of four of his friends who were going up a river a lot calmer than this one. It was the day before hunting season began and they were loaded down. Night fell faster than they expected. The watchman in front didn't take his job seriously. They hit a fallen tree trunk. The canoe headed straight for the bottom. The water was icy. The sky moonless. They were pulled straight down by the invisible vortex of the current. One of them never surfaced. The others, frozen, lost in the night, couldn't do anything for him.

We are quiet and vigilant the rest of the way. When we near the drop-off point, Herman cuts the motor, and our momentum carries us into a shallow spot some distance from it. I jump out and haul up the canoe. Nothing moving. Only the murmuring river and our hearts beating fast.

Maybe they're still there, Darès says, loading his weapon. We'll go through the woods and ambush them. They'll understand they've got no business hunting on our land.

We fall in behind him without a sound. We move around a silty stretch and soon see, through the trees, the cleared spot where our second dock is. Darès motions us to look for tracks. There are boot prints, no end of them. My family's eyes glitter with anger. Their faces harden. Diane waves her hand, ordering us to fan out and encircle the spot. I go where I am told to, mouth dry, muscles tense. The rifle I am carrying burns my fingers. I don't know who these people are, or what I have gotten myself into. I have no idea what my family is capable of. But I hide my doubts in the pit of my stomach, take up position in the dry leaves, and press my eye to the sight.

In the middle of the gravel are the remains of a fire with plastic bottles, cans, and packaging of all kinds. On the skirt of the woods, the two pickups and the van have their windows smashed and tires slashed. My muscles ease up. There is no one.

Then a shadow crosses my field of vision. My heart goes into high gear again. My hands shake on the rifle. Every small detail grabs my attention. Slowly, I get the better of my nerves. Probably just a false alarm, one blink of my eyelids too many, the hurried flight of a bird or a bounding squirrel, nothing more. I am about to let down my guard when I spot a coyote, its fur upright, its cheeks hollow, its eyes haggard. It senses our presence but does not make much of it. It is in the middle of licking its chops when a shot rings out. The animal collapses, its limbs splayed out unnaturally. Someone whistles three times. I stand up carefully and join my aunt and uncles on our dock.

Darès congratulates Diane on her perfect shot. But his smile quickly fades when he steps over to our vandalized vehicles.

We should have expected it, he says, a few tree branches on top weren't going to hide them forever.

We look around. The spot where the fire was, the garbage left behind. A tipped-over canoe in the brush. Darès says it is the same one we saw coming past us a while back. Not far from it, the grass is trampled. I follow the track and come upon a heap of bloody entrails. A crow lifts its eyes in my direction, caws spitefully, and flies off heavily. Green flies buzz. My family comes up behind me and gazes at the guts and tissue shining in the sun. No doubt about it, a moose was cleaned and quartered here.

They didn't even keep the heart or the liver or the kidneys, Diane says angrily, poking at the entrails with a stick. Judging from the size, I'd say it was a young male, a yearling.

While Herman inspects the pitiful state of his van, Darès paces the site in a rage. I step away to have a look at the logging road that crosses farther up, beyond our dock. Big rocks stick out everywhere and wide dried-up puddles make the road barely passable. No tire tracks on it. I wonder where they took the meat. When I go to turn back, I spot a narrow path leading into the mountains towards the Park.

I return to our group, my mind elsewhere. They are

talking, and they look serious. Behind them, the river slowly follows its course, the crow has returned to dig through the intestines, and trees wave in the breeze. Diane picks up the coyote and we move towards the canoe. A few steps later, four shots tear through the forest. In a panic, we hit the dirt and reach for our weapons. Darès is the only one standing. Smoke is issuing from the barrel of his rifle and he is wearing a smile. My ears are ringing so loudly I can't hear what he is saying. He points to the canoe in the brush. Four holes decorate the bottom.

We go downriver to the sound of the outboard backfiring. We keep our eyes on the bank that slips by as if it were the only thing moving. At the camp, everyone is full of questions. Darès explains what we saw. The discussion drags on as the twins circle around us with wooden swords. I am surprised Olio has not shown up. I ask Hesta where he is. My aunt glances at Sylvia. Their faces fall.

I don't know, Hesta answers, I thought he went with you.

AUGUST SECOND

I open my eyes to the morning light and the first thing I see is the empty bed next to me. I hurry downstairs. Everyone else is up. No one has seen Olio.

What's he up to? Darès wonders as he prepares for a day of hunting.

I don't know. I was hoping he'd come back during the night.

For a moment, the noisy morning routine goes silent. Even the twins look up from their bowls of oatmeal. I slump back on my chair. I don't know what to do.

He'll be back, Boccus assures me, don't worry.

Guilt has gotten the better of me.

We'll go for a walk in the woods, my aunt Hesta decides, trying to change my mood, you never know.

The thought gives me back some determination. The hunters say they will keep an eye out, too. I thank them, rush through breakfast, and leave with Hesta and Herman to scour the territory.

We start out by climbing the section of the mountain behind the camp to get a view of the valley. We follow a little stream, making a path for ourselves through wet ferns and dead trees lying across the forest floor. When the slope gets steeper, the stream divides and turns into a series of waterfalls. We move through the woody shadows. Behind the foliage we see the camp, the sinuous body of the river, and, in the distance, the peaks of the Park.

I call Olio's name several times. It fades into the valley, the echo weak and distant. My aunt and uncle do the same and we wait a moment, listening to the trees creaking together in the wind. Then we go our way.

Better than sitting back at the camp, waiting, but I don't think we'll find Olio this way. He isn't lost. He went away. And if he was out here somewhere, he'd simply watch us pass by.

AUGUST THIRD

I am standing on the little dock with Hesta. The boy has not come back yet. We turn our eyes to the fleeting movement of the river, the green shadows of the forest on the far bank, the line of mountains hooked to the sky.

The river is low. Green, grey, and bluish stones shine on the bottom. They fit together, one against the other, like the stones of ancient roads.

Olio can get along. He knows the forest better than anyone. He doesn't need anybody. But I curse myself for not being there to keep him from leaving. I take my head in my hands. My aunt comes and gently puts her arm around my shoulders.

It's good that you took care of him, she says, he needed it. But how long have you known him? Two months, not even?

I shrug. I can't answer.

Come on, my aunt urges me, taking me back with her towards the camp, go help out Sylvia. It'll do you good to work a little.

In the spot she prepared at the edge of the clearing, Sylvia shows me the borders of her garden. Several stumps need to be removed. I pick up the axe and begin the job. My aunt was right. My movements are smooth and free me from care. I put my mind to the blows raining down on the buried roots. Wood chips fly through the air. The stumps are stubborn; they won't give up the earth where they were born. When I hit a rock, the handle vibrates down to my bones. Sweat pearls on my forehead, runs down my skin, soaks my clothes. I lift my head to take a breather and see the twins playing hide-and-seek among the cords of wood. Their games don't last long, since there are only two of them. From time to time they stand stock still and look around, as if Olio might pop out and surprise them.

At day's end, I am exhausted. My hands are covered in blisters and I don't have the strength to think about anything. I half listen to my aunts and uncles talking over dinner. They make a list of what they need, insist on the importance of hunting, and subtly make fun of Sylvia's project.

When the generator goes off and the bulbs swallow their illumination, Janot lights a candle and sits down with an old magazine. I contemplate the shadowy room. The deck of cards glows on the shelf. Olio is gone, and his absence leaves a hole in me. I hold back my tears. Janot glances my way as he runs his fingers through the wavering flame. Long shadows leap across the room.

AUGUST FIFTH

I finish getting the Rototiller back in shape early in the afternoon. Janot is going to run it. The machine shakes him like a rag doll as it bites into the earth, jumping and bucking. He sets down rows between the stumps we could not pull out. In some places, the earth is ochre and almost sandy. Elsewhere, the humus has mixed with clods of clay that are grey and hard as asphalt.

Sylvia comes up next to me. She is pleased at how quickly the work is progressing.

If we add compost and cover it with tarps, she tells me, we'll have good soil for next year.

Next year – the words stick in my head. Next year might as well be centuries away. Sylvia asks me about Olio, then puts her hand on mine to console me. The Rototiller coughs black smoke and stalls for no reason. Janot looks back at us. I pull my hand away quickly, leave him with his engine problems, and return to the house as if my body weighed a ton.

Inside, Boccus is moving around the kitchen. He opens the cupboards, inspects the shelves, leaves no stone unturned.

We only have six bottles of mead left, he says, unnerved.

Herman comes into the room and teases him. Stop squirrelling away bottles for yourself. Boccus pretends he didn't hear. Herman sits down at the table, discouraged by another useless day scouring the woods.

Normally, in the summer, when we went out to maintain the trails, we came across moose all over the place.

I hear him, but don't listen. I am thinking about Olio. I hope he's all right. Wherever he is. I would hate myself if something happened to him. Herman pats me on the back when he sees how down I am. I scarcely have time to acknowledge his kindness when the twins come in and ask when their friend is coming back. My uncle wants to spare me the trouble of answering. He turns to them and starts telling a story. They sit down in front of him, calm and attentive.

A farmer had seven goats. One after the other, they ran away, up into the mountain, and ended up in the wolf's stomach. All except one. The farmer took the best care he could of her and gave her a wonderful green field with a clear stream running through it. At least, he said to himself, this is one goat that won't run away. The days went by and the goat started to get bored as she gazed at the mountain. She understood why her friends had run away. She envied them. The farmer understood what was on her mind. As angry as could be, he locked her up in the stable. The goat was sadder than ever. But in the stable, one window was half-open. She slipped out and headed for the mountain. Everything looked magnificent up there – the pine trees, the old oaks, the blue flowers, the juicy grass, the valley below. She played in the sun all day. When evening came, and she saw the light in the farmer's house far below, she wondered how she could have lived locked up for so long. Then the moon rose and a horrible howling echoed across the mountain.

Herman pauses, seeing how enchanted everyone is with his story. The twins are waiting for what will come next, their mouths open.

In the middle of the night, a branch snapped. It was the wolf. The goat stiffened and lowered her head, showing her horns. The wolf retreated a few steps and then, seeing how she hesitated, he took up his position again. He attacked once, and the goat defended herself fiercely. The struggle went on all through the night. As dawn broke, the goat had no more strength. Her willpower was not enough to change the way the world was made. So she lay down quietly in the grass, cold with the morning dew, and the wolf devoured her.

AUGUST SIXTH

The sky clouded over today. The thirsty vegetation is enjoying the break. The leaves reach out to gather every drop of humidity floating in the air.

It might seem a day like any other. Some go hunting, others have work around the camp. But since Olio disappeared, the sounds of morning, the voices, the chairs and the dishes in the room downstairs, everything is increasingly distant.

I am leaning on my shovel, vigorously mixing dead leaves with the dusty earth of the garden. The first drops splatter against my back. I straighten up and listen to the rain delicately striking the dry grass. Then the downpour is suddenly upon me; it catches me in the middle of the clearing like a scarecrow as the others head for shelter in the house.

The rest of the afternoon plays out between four walls, dangling conversations, the smell of the herb soup Sylvia is making, the twins' roughhousing. Outside, the rain is cutting the forest into vertical slices and beating on the roof. A storm might be brewing.

The hunters return one at a time, relieved to see a little rain. The soup is served. It looks delicious, but I am not very hungry. I examine the herbs floating in my bowl. Olio needed a little space, I tell myself. Maybe he had enough of me and my family. Since the beginning, he has irritated me with his stubbornness and his far-fetched stories, but I can't imagine myself without him.

The lights in the ceiling fixture dim, then flicker out. The darkness catches us off guard. The generator is out of gas. The rain is falling so hard we decide to light some candles. Thunder rolls in the distance.

Suddenly, a gust of wind blows into the room and snuffs out the candles. Olio has returned to the camp.

Everyone is surprised. They bombard him with questions. He pulls off his soaked jacket and sits down at the table, eyes averted. I want to run to him and take him in my arms, but I hold back. Better not to ask for too much. Hesta serves him a bowl of soup.

Here, start by eating. You'll tell us about it later.

Fascinated, the twins watch him devour everything on his plate. The wind and the rain whirl outside, and the water pouring off the gutter is deafening. I eat with one eye on Olio. Relief. My life has substance again. My little guy is back.

AUGUST SIXTH

And now, Darès asks Olio with a hint of wariness, tell us where you went.

The boy finishes his soup by lifting the bowl to his lips, then looks at my uncle coolly.

Out for a walk.

Darès doesn't buy it. He turns his head in the boy's direction. The storm rages and spits flashes of light over the forest.

I look at Olio's jacket on the back of the chair. Water is slowly dripping onto the floor. The cut of the jacket and its logo are unfamiliar.

Where did you sleep all those nights? I push him, determined to find out more.

In the pines, where else?

You didn't meet anybody? Darès asks, losing patience.

No, Olio tells him, scratching his head, nobody. But I saw moose tracks on the way back down. They looked fresh.

My aunts and uncles do not react. The silence in the room buzzes. My family expects me to be firmer with him. I am supposed to play my role. A child can't just disappear like that for days without having to explain. But I know that the more you insist, the more you get bogged down in his lies.

In any case, Darès says drily as lightning fractures the sky behind him, I hope you're telling the truth.

It is getting late. Beyond the walls of this room, the storm shakes the great cedars. We put the discussion off until tomorrow and repair to our quarters. I am back in the darkness of the attic with Olio. Janot lingers downstairs as he often does.

You've got a new jacket, I say in a low voice.

Not bad, don't you think?

Where did you get it?

It doesn't matter, he points out. You're the only one who noticed.

The joy I felt when he returned has burned off entirely and I find it hard not to lose patience. I turn over in bed and wait, pretending to be weary of his stories.

If you want to know, Olio finally decides to tell me, I went to the dock through the woods. On the way I found a trail that leads up to the Park. You know what? It goes directly to the Station without passing by the gate or taking the ridge. If we'd known, we could have gone that way!

I sit up in bed. A flash of lightning illuminates the attic. Olio smiles; he is happy to have my attention.

It's true, there are guards, he goes on, but they're not around the Station, they're positioned at the entrance to the buildings. I even managed to slip by them and get into one of the hotels. Inside, people are going from one door to the next, their clothes are clean, the corridors smell like food. And the view is spectacular from the top floor. Up there, you're above the forest. You can see the ski slopes, the summit with the burned-out building, even the lookout where we stopped. But after a while, the guards caught me and threw me out.

Did you stay there the whole time?

Yes, he tells me. Most of the time I spent in the camps outside the hotels. There's all kinds of people, hundreds of them maybe, living one on top of the other in tents and under tarps. There's garbage lying around, camping equipment, clothes drying everywhere. The kids are always fighting.

The adults look exhausted. The hunters coming back from the woods are even worse. But at least, there, no one asked me any questions. You know where I slept? In the yellow float plane in the river!

Tell me, I interrupt him, what were you looking for?

I don't know, he admits, hesitating. Maybe my parents ended up there.

The storm has blown itself out and the moon is rising. Its grey light reaches our room and I see disappointment in Olio's small dark eyes. I go to him and hold him in my arms. He buries his face in my shoulder and cries.

In the misty sky, a single cloud chases the storm. The cloud passes in front of the moon like the shadow of a hand in front of someone's face.

I'm happy to see you again, I say softly. I was afraid you wouldn't come back.

Olio clings to me tighter. I am crying, too. When Janot comes up to the attic, we go back to our beds and are quiet, as if nothing had been spoken.

AUGUST SEVENTH

One of the tall cedars, the one that was leaning over, was knocked down by the storm last night. Strangely, no one remembers hearing the heavy shock of its fall or the ground trembling under the impact. But this morning, we pause to think of this giant that fell a few steps from the house.

The tree is even more imposing on the ground. The wrinkled skin of its trunk, its crooked branches, its head still full of sky. It left a great empty place in the canopy. Already the saplings are gorging themselves on the light that was forbidden them.

A minute later, the chainsaws are screaming as they throw off grey-blue clouds of smoke. We cut up the giant fallen cedar. We pile the branches to carry them near the firepit and quickly stack the logs. Several times the saws backfire, cough, then stall out. Darès turns and gives me a look.

That's because the gas has gone off, I tell him. The carburetors foul up fast.

My uncle pretends he didn't hear me and yanks on the starter cord for all he's worth. To my surprise, he is able to get the motor going again. He idles it at full speed and dares me to say something.

We finish just before noon and everyone goes back to the tasks at hand. My aunts and uncles go hunting, Janot plays schoolteacher, Sylvia and I pull rocks out of a section of the garden. It's as if the tree had never fallen. The troops' morale is a little less brilliant by day's end. Summer is going by, we still don't have a moose, and our supplies of oil, noodles, and rice grow lower by the day.

We'll have to depend on small game, Hesta decides, trying to sound reassuring.

It's better than waiting for a garden, Darès mutters, looking at Sylvia and me.

Olio interrupts my uncle and says he wants to go hunting.

Start by doing what you're told, comes the answer.

Boccus stands up, tired of his brother acting like he is everyone's father. He suggests we play cards. Heads nod. Why not?

Don't be a sore loser this time, all right? Darès warns Olio.

That's enough. I step in to cool things off. Don't make such a big deal out of it.

The game begins. Cards slip across the table, money changes hands, curses fly. I am part of every hand, but deep down, I am very far from what is happening around me.

I have this lingering feeling that everyone at the table is playing a role, and can't step out of the character that has been assigned them. That our exchanges are orchestrated according to a particular mechanism. That our insistence on hunting and domestic work saves us while alienating us. As if our way of living was a form of voluntary penitence. I wonder what we're doing here, away from the world, shipwrecked sailors, prisoners of a sea of green.

Darès pounds the table. I jump. It's my turn. I get myself together. The cards change hands, luck turns sour, strategies diverge. Olio's face shines after he wins a small sum from Diane. A few games later, I start believing in my luck and the possibility of winning big. The back of my head is itching. I try to force things and lose a considerable amount. My rage boils over. Olio watches my reaction, discreetly enjoying himself. It's all I can do to keep from throwing the cards on the floor and jumping up from the table.

AUGUST SIXTEENTH

Sunday. We do the calendar routine with a carefully measured dose of mead. One week is like the next and the one before. The forest is ungenerous and the hunters are slowly losing their cool. Darès accuses Olio of making up the story of moose tracks on the mountain. The boy tells my uncle that he could just as well give his spot to him.

Before Darès can react, I announce I'm going with him. I feel like hunting, too. It's been a while.

The twins follow the exchange, envious, scratching their scalps.

Fine, my blind is yours, Darès tells me, watching the light refract in his glass, as long as you bring back a moose.

We have a problem, Sylvia informs us, standing behind her children.

We look up.

The twins have lice.

No one says anything. The afternoon has just been turned upside down. We all begin scratching our heads, discouraged.

Darès asks how they could have caught them.

It doesn't matter, Hesta tells him, the main thing is to fix the problem.

I glance at Olio with his mop of messy hair and his new jacket. He couldn't care less about lice, he just wants to go hunting tomorrow.

We leap into action and the operation takes us until evening. Our sheets and pillowcases are steeping in kettles of boiling water. The electric razor and the generator know no rest. Our blond, black, grey, and white hair falls to the ground and ends up in the fire. Even Sylvia's curls and my uncles' tangled beards are sacrificed. The twins can't believe what they look like and scream about how disgusting burning hair smells. Hesta prepares a mixture of oil and vinegar and we rub our scalps with it. We rinse our heads, put away the washing, and make our beds. Night has fallen by the time we sit down at the table, worn thin by the task. We look at each other under the hanging ceiling lamps. With our short hair, our features are sharper and stand out in shocking clarity.

We look like a band of warriors, Darès says.

More like prisoners in a work camp, Janot adds.

AUGUST SEVENTEENTH

Since dawn, we have been in the blind, watching the marsh. The little wooden construction is high on a platform attached to a tree. When the wind blows, the blind swings with the rest of the forest, and we let it rock us.

Olio calls a few times, hands around his mouth. Every time the leaves stir, he squirms on his chair, convinced a moose is about to appear. Despite our recent failures, the landscape seems full of promise. Olio takes my gun and looks through the sight. He scans the shadowy spots beneath the trees.

Boom, he says softly. All around, time surrounds and besieges us.

Yet it's good to be away from work. Join the slowness of things. Waiting instead of getting things done.

I'm happy to be with my family. I couldn't have gone anywhere else. But still, I wonder what I have come in search of here. I feel like I'm wearing a mask of routine and slowly disappearing behind the tasks I am meant to accomplish. Something eludes me in what we are becoming. Day after day, we hunt, we break our backs, we fight for a thin ray of light stolen from the forest. And we redo the calendar week after week without knowing when we are going to get out of here.

Olio and I are slumped back on the old car seats. My rifle is leaning on the edge of the shooting window. The woods are still. It is probably past noon. It's hard to say; daylight has barricaded itself behind the grey belly of the clouds. The only glow is from the foliage, the plants, the grass around us. As if they were the sky.

Some kind of animal is skipping across the spongy roof of our lookout. A squirrel. We hear it scolding, complaining, sounding its high-pitched call. When it shows up at the edge of the window, Olio waves at it and it leaps into the void.

Then I hear a vague sound. Twigs breaking beneath the weight of hooves. My senses grow sharp, as if someone had flipped a switch in a dark room. I watch and wait. Not another sound. I turn to Olio. He hasn't noticed anything. Maybe I was dreaming, my imagination playing tricks on me. I return to the empty-headed observation of the forest. The absence of talk is intoxicating. The stagnant water of the marsh is a dark mirror shot through with the weight of dead tree trunks. The vegetation is dense and the more I watch it, the more a veil falls over it. I am growing numb, my eyes are closing, I fight sleep but it triumphs and my chin falls to my chest. Images of luxuriant forests, animals of splendour, skies from the end of the world, tangled under my eyelids. Then all of a sudden, a gunshot tears at my eardrums.

I leap to my feet, my heart pounding. Olio is standing next to me, still sighting the gun. He quickly reloads and takes up position. The empty casing shines on the old plywood floor. I look out every angle our shooting window offers; the marsh is calm and deserted.

What's happening?

I got him. I'm sure I did, but he went up the side of the mountain. Come on, let's go see.

AUGUST SEVENTEENTH

No, I order him, taking back the gun, we'd better wait. He'll go to ground and bleed out. If we take off after him now, he'll know we're on his trail and he'll hide in the woods until he collapses. Then we'll lose him.

Olio says nothing. It takes all his strength to wait. I put my eye to the sight. A plume of mist hangs over the marsh, above the cattails, blurring my view of the forest.

Where was he?

Olio points to a grove of pines standing over the muddy water. I look for tracks on the ground reddened by fallen needles. But the spot is too far away, and with the humidity, my sight is fogged over.

You sure you got him?

We turn and look at each other. His smile is stronger than my doubts.

We patient it out. Olio can hardly sit still. I motion him to calm down, but like the other times, he runs off before I can hold him back. I close my eyes; it's once too many. I figure we have about four hours of daylight left. I go after him, bent over and making as little noise as possible. On the ground, blood and tracks lead up towards the mountain.

I can't believe it, and neither can Olio. I congratulate him, then follow the track of the wounded moose. At first the going is easy, but the terrain changes. The bloodstains fade. We look for clues. A branch snaps underfoot. We stop. The same sound, again. Like footsteps. I motion

Olio to hide back against a tree alongside me. I slip the safety off the rifle and turn around slowly. I see movement through the branches just below. I squint, it's not a moose, four men are slipping through the brush. I don't know what they're doing there, I figure they heard our shot and they're after the same moose we are. I don't move a muscle. We don't have safety vests. If we take off, they could end up shooting at us.

Olio pulls on my sleeve and points the opposite way, into the trees.

The moose, he whispers, the moose went that way, come on.

He pulls me along through the woods. I glance behind. The other hunters are invisible. We push our way through the thickets. The weir of young shoots is so dense they stop us cold. We turn around and the moose is there, right in front of us, among the branches. It stares at us with hollow eyes. I see blood from the wound glowing on its chest. Its breathing is laboured but it is still standing.

Olio reaches out. He wants the gun. I push him aside and motion him to hold still. I brace myself on one knee and aim at the animal in the underbrush. I have a perfect view of its flank. As I slowly move the crosshairs of the sight to just behind its shoulder, I think of the men prowling the woods and I freeze.

What are you doing? Olio demands, impatient. Go ahead and shoot!

No more hesitating. I squeeze the trigger.

Two pheasants rise up and fly away. The moose's body shivers. It takes a step or two, then collapses noisily in the brush. Olio is already running towards it. I follow; it is an impressive heap of rough fur with splayed legs, its neck bent skyward and tongue stuck out. Its eyes are wide open and lightless. A young male, two years old or so with a small set of uneven antlers.

We're happy, we can't wait to show our aunts and uncles. We stand still a moment, hypnotized by the majestic animal deformed by death.

Then I move into action. I pull out my knife and bleed the moose, slitting its throat down to the jugular. Next I have to empty it. It's been years. I squat down next to its enormous belly and draw a line to open it from its sternum to its neck. Olio helps me by lifting one of its front legs. I remember every step now as my hands disappear into its blood, fur, and fat. I can practically hear Darès and Diane telling me how to proceed for the thousandth time. I open the intestinal wall, cut the tendons of the pelvis, pull on the trachea, split the ribs, thrust my arms into its chest cavity, detach the diaphragm, and pull out the organs with my bare hands. Olio looks on, amazed.

I am gathering up the liver, heart, and kidneys from the steaming entrails when I hear someone coughing, announcing their presence. I look up. The four guys we spotted are watching us, their arms crossed. One of them has his foot on my rifle and the other three have surrounded us. Olio doesn't react. I stand up, keeping my knife flat against my leg. The four of them are expressionless. They are clothed in old shirts and torn pants. The dark circles under their eyes stand out against their anemic skin. The guy in front of me is the runt of the group. His cheeks are hollow and his eyebrows all but cover his eyes.

It's our moose now, he declares.

I think it over. Outside of my weapon on the ground, I think they have only one rifle. We are fifteen minutes or so from the marsh. Not far. At the camp, they heard our shot, that's for sure. They must already be on their way.

Don't try and play the hero, the runt tells us, just move on.

I look down, trying to stall for time.

Did you come from the Station? Olio asks.

The runt stares at him coldly.

Us, too. Except we left.

The four men stare at Olio, then me, then they shrug.

So what?

We can share the animal, Olio proposes, taking a step towards them. Half-half. You'll never be able to carry it all, anyway.

We turn to gauge the impressive, bloody carcass sprawled out in the grass. One of the guys talks to the runt, scratching his scalp furiously.

Okay, half is two quarters, and if we take turns carrying them, we'll get back tomorrow morning. Otherwise, with this heat we might end up with spoiled meat and it won't be worth anything.

A deal? I ask.

The runt looks at his troops, then Olio. He nods.

All right. But finish what you were doing and cut it up in quarters. We'll choose the pieces we want.

The grey sky is beginning to loosen. Relieved, I bend over the moose, make a cut at the base of its neck, lift the skin, reach down to the bone, and twist the head until it breaks off. Then I move along the last ribs, insert the tip of the blade between two vertebrae, and separate the front and the back of the animal. All I need to do next is free a set of ribs from the spinal column and we'll have a head and four large sections of meat.

I take a break and look around. No sign of my family. Maybe they are waiting for us to come to them. Maybe it's better that way. We take our share, they take theirs, and that's it.

At the camp, we'll tell them a bear stole two quarters from us, Olio whispers to me.

We'll have to come up with something, I agree.

The runt stands next to me, evaluating the quarters. His bushy eyebrows droop. Satisfied with my work, he hands me back my rifle and offers me a roll-your-own.

AUGUST SEVENTEENTH

Three gunshots shake the forest. We duck and wait for the echo to pass, then panic sets in. Olio runs in my direction. The moose quarters fall to the ground. Everyone is confused. I hear voices. The guys with the runt, then farther away but more assertive, my family.

Before I know it, Darès steps forward, reloading his gun, with his brothers and sisters behind. In no time, the four intruders are surrounded by a bloodthirsty pack with their hands on their weapons. I feel the chambers of my heart contracting and expanding with painful precision. The runt is trying to figure out what is going on. He is the only one of his group who is armed. They can't stand up to us.

Get out of here! Darès yells. Get out now! This is our land!

I grab Olio by the arm and lead him away before things degenerate.

We agreed to share the meat, Olio pipes up.

My aunts and uncles stare at us. What we are saying makes no sense.

Who killed the moose? Diane asks.

We did, Olio and I answer.

The guys claim we're lying. Darès walks up to the runt, his anger at the boiling point.

You've got an agreement? With who? Them? my uncle points his chin in our direction. The only one you can make agreements with is me. And I'm telling you to go back where you came from, right now.

The runt looks at me, bitterness on his face. I'm caught in the middle, but there's nothing I can do.

It's better if you leave, I say, ashamed.

We need that meat, the runt insists, his voice trembling.

Darès has had enough. He slams the butt of his rifle into his stomach. The runt falls backward into his friends' arms. Olio steps forward and puts himself between them and my family. Darès pushes him out of the way with a storm of insults, grabs the runt's rifle, and pulls out the bullets. It's Olio's turn to fly into a rage.

One of their kids needs medicine, I try and explain.

I suppose you believe what people tell you? my uncle cuts me off.

The runt gets his legs back underneath him. He and his group palaver in low voices, then retreat, cursing us. I watch them fade into the indifferent forest and wonder what we have become. When they have disappeared from my field of vision, I go back to my family. They are rubbing their hands over the quartered animal. They congratulate us and slap us on the back.

That means I'll be going back to Marchand's soon, Herman says, his face shining.

It's great to kill a moose, Darès points out, but giving half of it away to people who trespass on our land and that we don't even know, what went through your mind? You might as well invite them to our camp!

No one comments. Everyone is too busy with the carcass.

We've been waiting for a kill like this for a long time, Boccus adds, trying to lighten the atmosphere. This calls for a celebration, if you ask me.

With Herman, they carry the head and two quarters on

the stretcher they brought. They move towards the camp, breathing hard, climbing through the darkness and underbrush. Hesta gathers up the organs I set aside. Diane keeps an eye out to make sure the four guys don't try and follow us.

Where's Olio now? Darès wants to know. His nerves are still frayed.

I notice his absence, too. I whistle three times and he shows up a few minutes later with no explanation as my uncle and I are each hefting a quarter on our shoulders.

The night is pitch-black by the time we reach the clearing. Boccus and Herman are waiting for us, in a heap on the porch. We barely have time to recover from our work when Diane orders us to get the generator going, plug in the lamps, take out the folding table, and bring some wet cloths. Sylvia and Janot look after preparing the organ meat. We scrape down the quarters, wash them, and wrap them in cheesecloth. Then we hang them in the shed and make sure the locks are tight.

And sit down at the table like famished ogres and fall upon the slices of liver and onions that my cousin sets down before us.

The flesh is dark red, almost black, with a delicious taste of pine. But the morose atmosphere around the table does not lift. A few words, but mostly the sound of chewing. The words are few, without purpose, not a real conversation.

We've got two bottles of mead left! Boccus announces, trying to light a spark, his face florid.

The honey alcohol sparkles in our glasses, but we drink in silence. Something is stuck in our craws. Even Olio and the twins are quiet.

After another glass, my aunts and uncles recover their enthusiasm. They begin planning Herman's next trip to Marchand's.

It's about time, they all agree, naming what we need. Flour, potatoes, oil, salt, batteries, wool for knitting, fresh vegetables, coffee if there is any, and, most of all, mead.

Olio and I have nothing to say. It's like the others don't even know we're in the room. There is still a score to settle with those people from the Station, but for now the subject is off limits. At one point the light flickers in the camp, turns yellow, then gives way to darkness. The generator is acting up again.

Just as well, Diane tells us, getting to her feet. It's late and we've got a lot of meat to fix tomorrow.

That evening, I lie down and realize again that I have no idea what is happening at the Station or anywhere else. And even here, between my family's reign and Olio's trickery, I don't know which way to turn.

AUGUST EIGHTEENTH

Boccus puts a kettle on the fire, Herman sharpens the knives, Hesta takes the key to the shed from the hook by the door. We go with her to pick up the smokehouse grills, the glass jars, the salt, and set up our operation in the clearing with our treasure of meat.

We have three or four days' work ahead of us. We will salt the best pieces, cut the rest into strips for smoking or cubes for preserving. My aunts and uncles are consistent, like precision machines. They slice through the flesh, following the lines of muscle, as if their knife blades knew exactly where to go. The twins have a job, too: chasing away the flies. They circle the table with cedar branches.

That's quite the moose you two got, Darès admits, considering the quality of the meat laid out before us. But let's be clear about it, the meat we kill is for us and no one else. We're a family of eleven. Sylvia has two young kids. If we want to be in good shape this winter, and we all want that, we need every animal we can kill.

A frown crosses our faces at the thought of winter. I nod. I know Darès is right. But a doubt lingers. Those people needed the meat, too.

No one comments. Everyone rallies behind Darès's opinion and we go back to work. Two magpies watch us from their spot in a tree. As soon as we have our backs turned, they leave their perch and grab a piece of meat. Olio tries to frighten them away. They stare him down, unimpressed, whistle a note or two, and go back to waiting for another chance.

In the afternoon, I am alone in the main room, busy cooking the meat for preserving. I thrust the glass containers into boiling water, wait, then pull them out and start with another set. My eyes wander the steamy room. The natural lustre of the wood has changed with time and everything seems darker than I remember it from childhood. In these four walls, I feel like I'm in a deep cave decorated with a few meaningless objects. A deck of cards, a calendar, a dusty set of moose antlers.

Soon, several dozen jars are cooling on the counter. If I listen carefully, I can hear the clicking of the metal tops that seal tight like suction cups. I think of the moose we killed. It was a big animal standing on four legs, and now it is food in little containers.

Sylvia comes into the room and pulls me from my thoughts. The steam whirls around her and dances in the light that falls on her shaved hair, her neck, and shoulders.

Are the jars ready? she asks, coming to my side.

Her green eyes are so open to me, so true, so close, I can't help but fall into them. She slips a hand under my shirt.

What are you doing? I ask helplessly.

Her laughter is pure temptation and our bodies draw together, moved by magnetic force, an underground current.

The door to the room opens. We pull away like lovers in reverse. Boccus and Hesta stare at us for a moment, then tell us it's time to clean up. We'll start again tomorrow. They leave with the boxes of jarred meat.

We meet in the clearing when the cleaning is done and the padlock put on the shed door. It was a good day's work and there are two more quarters to prepare. We have meat now, and my aunts and uncles feel reassured. The incident with the hunters from the Station has faded and the atmosphere is festive again. The sun is following its inevitable path behind the mountains. The crest of the tall cedars is illuminated by warm, yellow light above the shadowy zone where we dwell. Next to me, Olio is pensive. Hand over his eyes, he is watching the evening sky. Suddenly he raises his arm and points to something in the distance. I scan the horizon and spot a thick column of smoke curling above the forest. He moves into the clearing.

Fire! he shouts. There's a fire!

My aunts and uncles glance at one another. It's too big for a campfire. They are afraid the wind will rise and spread it.

It's for real, Olio insists, we should go and see! We have to put it out!

The twins are waving and pointing. Everyone gets moving; they're afraid of what will happen if the forest burns. Herman and Boccus grab shovels and pails and head for the source of the smoke, and the rest of the family follows. Darès catches my arm.

You stay here with me.

I look at him. His face is ashen. In the clearing, Olio is waving at us to come, too. When he sees we're not going anywhere, he gives up and disappears into the forest with the others.

My uncle and I are hypnotized by the scrolls of smoke that wheel through the air on the wind.

My blind must be burning, he says, worried, then goes to get his rifle. It can't be anything but that.

I hear something behind me. I barely have time to turn around. Someone twists my arm behind my back and pins me face down to the ground. I fight, but it's no use, I'm a prisoner.

I call out to my uncle, trying to figure out what's happening. I see him – three wild-eyed guys are disarming him. It happens fast. Darès tries to explain, he wants dialogue, negotiation. His words come to an abrupt halt when he gets kicked in the crotch. He drops to the ground, gasping for breath as the three men fall on him.

I shout and fight and struggle to get free. When I manage to flip over and see my assailant, I get a face full of knuckles and everything goes black.

AUGUST EIGHTEENTH

I wake up to the humming of the generator. I open my eyes. I am lying on the ground in the wet grass. The lights of the house and the shed glow in the night. Hesta and Boccus are standing above me. They help me sit up. My head is pounding violently. I touch my forehead and feel the wound on my eyebrow.

I look around. Olio is in the clearing, off to one side. Diane is standing in the shed door, discouraged. Darès is sitting on the steps, a compress on the back of his head. He is talking with Herman. When our eyes meet, he slowly gets to his feet and moves towards me, holding his ribs.

They got us good, but I didn't black out. I saw it all. Your friends from yesterday. They took everything they could and ran back into the woods.

And they burned the blind by the marsh, Diane adds.

I'm still woozy and it takes me some time to understand what's going on.

I picture the charred springs of the two car seats among the ruins of the blind.

Come on, Darès tells me sharply, call your kid. We're going to settle this inside.

Hesta and Boccus support me until I can stand on my own. Olio follows us in, head down, and we join the others. I lift my head and look at my grandfather's moose trophy hanging on the wall. It keeps watch over our isolated, fragile little world. Olio is at my side. He stares at his hands on his thighs, no reaction, even when voices are raised around him.

They stole a rifle, two boxes of jarred moose, some smoked fish, and three cans of gas, Diane reports.

They took us by surprise, Darès admits, but what's strange is how they knew exactly where the shed key was. Like someone had told them.

All eyes are on Olio and me. The table is like a giant space that cannot be crossed. I look into their faces and feel like a complete stranger. Even Sylvia seems to have her doubts.

We have nothing to do with it, I answer, touching the wound on my forehead. What do you want us to say?

My family will blame me no matter what I say. They are looking for a scapegoat.

You know, Olio tells Darès insolently, that's what happens when you try to keep everything for yourself.

The slap hits Olio a second later. The sound of flesh is sharp and dry. Olio takes it without flinching. Not me. I jump on Darès and grab him by the collar. He struggles and frees his fists. Herman and Boccus get between us. Hesta yells. We freeze when we see each other's faces, the veins standing out on our necks and foreheads. You're in bad enough shape as it is, Diane tells us. We go back to our chairs. I look at Olio. He is rubbing his cheek and his eyes dart left and right as if looking for a way out.

No one wants to be the first to speak. The twins are trying to understand what's happening. They press against their mother. Olio goes up to the attic without a word, but Darès's anger is not appeased.

Tell me, what kind of game is that kid playing? Who does he think we are? If you had a little more authority over him, we wouldn't be in this mess.

I think we should have shared the meat, too, I state firmly.

Everyone has their needs. What good is it to act like there's nobody in this world but us?

Darès's face turns purple. His brothers try in vain to calm him down.

How do you think we're going to get through the next six months? Herman is going to go beg for charity from Marchand? I'm the oldest here and I decide. If the way we live bothers you, he thunders, as if nothing could stop him, remember we're not forcing anyone to stay here. Just ask Nep.

Faces darken as my uncle's absence fills the room.

What you two don't understand, Darès continues, is that now that those people saw our supplies of food and fuel, they'll be back, you can count on it.

A storm of comments and opinions fills the room.

And if it's not them, it'll be others. This won't be the same forest anymore. We'll have to patrol the woods and keep watch at night. No one's going to take advantage of us. Not them, not anybody else.

Then what? It's my turn to lose control. We're going to build a fortress? That makes no sense!

That's enough! Hesta shouts. Shut up, you two!

My aunt stares at us, mute chagrin in her eyes. No one can bear the silence that follows. Slowly we each go our separate ways, relieved to put off the final outcome.

All that for a little meat and some spoiled gas, I tell myself, at a loss, touching my wound delicately.

Boccus stops me as I am about to join Olio in the attic.

Tomorrow morning, you and your kid are coming with me to the lake for a few days. We'll go fishing. And let the others take the time they need to settle down. We leave at first light.

AUGUST NINETEENTH

We head up to the lake through the forest still soaked with night. This early, only the birds believe a new day is coming. We follow the sinuous route of the trail. The landscape changes as we leave the camp behind. My forehead is not too painful and my knee is holding up. But I am still struck by what happened last evening. I talk to Olio about it. He maintains he didn't do anything wrong. That Darès and I should have come to the marsh with him and the others to contain the fire. I listen and put one foot after the other, dazzled by Olio's impudence, though I don't believe things could have happened any differently. In the morning sky, a scattering of red-winged blackbirds chases after two crows, stabbing at them with their beaks.

We reach the shelter made of old tarps just before noon. We settle in, bail out the rain water accumulated in the aluminum rowboat, and with a few strokes, slip silently over the mirrored surface of the lake.

Our destination is the entrance to a little stream surrounded by gnarled pines. Long garlands of blue and green moss hang from the branches. The soft voice of the water tells us that the stream is flowing among the reeds. We tie on our bobbers and drop our lines in. The breeze toys with our thoughts, the boat turns lazily on its anchor, and from time to time a loon's lengthy incantation echoes and fades.

I watch Olio fish. His concentration is moving. He looks like a young sailor with his short blond hair filled with light, his clothes that are too small for him, and his sharp eyes. I am wondering more and more how a boy like him could find any interest living like a recluse with a hard-headed and possessive family like mine. What awaits us here? Can I offer him something better?

Olio calls out, triumphant, as he brings up his first trout. Boccus is in the mood to celebrate, and my questions go unanswered.

By afternoon, the bottom of the boat is covered with fish. It is time to go back to shore. As I am reeling in, my rod practically bends in two and my line traces wide circles running downward. My rod creaks as I try and fight back. Suddenly, the trout leaps from the water, breaks the quiet of the evening, and heads for the depths, pulling all the line it can. The battle lasts a good while. My arms tire. When we spot the silver reflection just below the surface, Olio leans over the edge of the boat and grabs the trout by the gills, his hand quick and merciless. We admire the heft of its round, orange-tinted belly and its curving mouth and wide fins.

We could feed an army with it, Boccus declares, weighing the fish in his hands.

A sly smile plays on his face, and without warning my uncle throws the fish back into the water. The waves spread out across the surface, then disappear. I can't believe it.

What's the matter? Boccus asks. Like your kid said, we can't keep everything for ourselves.

Behind me, Olio laughs. I don't know what to think as I pull up anchor. We return, hypnotized by the shivering light of the water disturbed by our progress. A few hours later, our catch is eviscerated and protected from tomorrow's heat by a thick cover of pine boughs. When night falls, Olio goes into the shelter, dreaming of tomorrow's fish. Boccus produces a bottle of mead from his bag; it comes from his secret stash, he says. We sit on the shore and watch the fog gathering along the banks. He passes me the bottle and I take a good gulp. Its warmth is soothing and I feel at one with this place of islands, trees, and water.

The days are getting shorter, Boccus remarks, turning up the collar of his shirt. We're on the downhill slope of summer.

He speaks the truth. I dread the moment when cold and snow will force us into confinement in the camp. I take another drink, but it is swallowing me.

We're just pawns on the great chessboard of the woods, my uncle goes on. What happened yesterday won't change anything in the long run. You know, the forest is implacable, the camp is small, and the winters are long. There's no use cursing the blackout. It's like family. You fight so nothing will change and you stick together and tear each other to shreds. I can't believe we're still living under the same roof. In the same house of cards. When I see how things are going with us, sometimes I figure Nep was right to head for the coast.

My uncle counts his last cigarettes, then offers me one. We smoke and commend ourselves to the depths of the night.

I've got only one thing to say, he sums up, finishing the mead. There's still time. You need to get away from us.

AUGUST TWENTY-THIRD

After the morning's fishing, we haul the rowboat back to the edge of the woods and start down the path towards the camp, loaded like mules. Olio leads the way. I watch him opening the trail and go back to my thoughts. What will life at the camp be like after the fight we had? Maybe Boccus is right. It's time to leave. But where to? I have no idea of the state of the world outside of our little piece of forest.

We reach the clearing by midday. The great cedars look like giants tired of holding up the sky. Everyone is busy with their chores around the shed. They are preparing for the next trip to Marchand's.

Herman is going tomorrow, Darès informs us when we arrive. We're going to round out the load with part of our reserves. The canoe won't be full, but that's the way it is. You should know we put bear traps by the dock. If those people come back, they're in for a surprise.

Olio stares at my uncle with steely eyes. He sets down his share of the fish on the ground and walks over to Janot, who is reading. I consider my uncle with a combination of incomprehension and disgust, but he pays no attention. The wound above my eye is healing nicely, he tells me. We're made tough in this family.

My aunt Diane comes over, sharpening a filleting knife. We spread out our catch on the work table and start preparing the trout with a few brief words about the weather and the unusual behaviour of the game.

In the evening, Hesta serves the heart of our moose in thin slices. The texture is dense and the flesh is delicious. We devour it in a matter of minutes like birds in winter. And then, like every Sunday, we gather around the calendar to make up the schedule for the coming week. Cut wood to rebuild the blind by the marsh. Visit our other hunting spots. Sweep the chimney. Prepare the food. Take care of the twins. Clean the engines.

Everything whirls around in my head, and it hits me when I realize how quickly my family has gone back to normal. How nothing can shake their will to continue as they have always done. I wonder what I'm doing here. What I'm waiting for. Hoping for. I am like a man holding his breath as he searches for escape from a dark icy lake. I run my hands nervously over the edge of the table and see that Olio has carved his name among the other traces. I look in his direction. He smiles and goes up to the attic with Janot. Boccus searches the kitchen in hopes of finding a bottle of mead. Herman tells him to relax, he'll be bringing more back soon.

I know this can't go on. Neither for Olio nor for me. I need to make a decision before we bog down here and winter catches us. I gather my courage. It is time to discreetly ask Herman if Olio and I can come with him to Marchand's tomorrow.

My uncle nods slowly as if he weren't the least surprised.

I told you so, Darès whispers to him, didn't I?

Diane turns towards me, her face frozen with disappointment that she works very hard not to show.

What's come over you? Hesta bursts out, staring at me, tears in her eyes. You can't do that. Think of Olio! Where are you taking him? We're not doing so bad here. We're a family. Even I'm staying here instead of going to Luperc.

I can hear myself being torn in two. I take my aunt's

hand a moment, then get to my feet. I hold their gaze as I go out on my own.

I walk to the middle of the clearing. The muted rumble of the generator hangs in the air like an old dream. The garden is just a few rows of poor earth among the rotting stumps. Farther on, the trees are a dark veil, a wall to walk through. When the light goes off in the house and silence settles between the sounds of the night, Sylvia appears next to me.

This place is a continuous uproar, and you know it. No one can escape it, but everything will work out, trust me. Olio and the twins get along pretty well, don't you think? And if you go, who will help me with the garden?

A gibbous moon pulls itself above the line of the forest. Its light cuts through the cover of the trees and its shadow play casts lace at our feet. Sylvia presses against me. We stay like that for a while, watching clouds cross the sky like lost wanderers. When I feel her warm lips on my neck, my desire grows too strong. I take a deep breath, draw my head away, and resist her green eyes burning in the night. When I pull her hand from my hip and move away slowly, only her voice holds fast to me.

Please don't leave!

I go up to the attic, my mind made up, and begin getting my things ready. My tarp, changes of clothes, sleeping bag. My eyes meet the pile of mattresses in the corner. The space around me shrinks as I imagine the long, sleepless winter nights, side by side with the others.

I look over at Olio. His bag is packed. He and Janot are consulting the map by candlelight. My cousin turns to me.

Is it true? You're leaving for the coast? You think the villages there are hooked up to wind turbines? Really, I don't know how long we can hold out here, but when there's no more gas, our aunts and uncles won't be the bosses anymore.

But I don't care, I'm sick of this place, sick of doing what I'm supposed to as they go on with their nitpicking. Calendar, meat, forest – I can't take it anymore. Tomorrow morning, that's it, I'm going with you.

Janot goes back to his bed and pulls the covers over his head. Olio gives me a sly look and packs the map in his bag, then blows out the candle.

I lie down, completely exhausted but unable to sleep. I think of Sylvia raising her two children here – how long has it been? Okay, she's not doing too bad, but what's the point of living as recluses? Where will that get us? The night comes creeping in through the open window. Beyond the clearing, sounds rise up. Animals squealing, bellowing, crying out. Beasts coupling or tearing each other apart, it's hard to know the difference.

AUGUST TWENTY-FOURTH

Everyone is up when I come down from the attic with my bag. They pretend not to notice the tense atmosphere. It could almost be an ordinary morning. Boccus making oatmeal, the twins fighting over a spot next to Olio, Darès and Diane talking in front of the window. Herman is noting down everyone's requests and making calculations on a piece of paper.

The sun has risen above the tops of the tall cedars by the time we finish loading the canoe. The motor dangles from the back between two gas cans. There's a little room between the jars of meat and sacks of smoked fish.

I pick up my walking sticks from exactly where I left them when I came to this place. I call Olio. He comes running with his bag across his chest. We take one last look at the camp with its backdrop of vegetation, its roof covered with moss, and its triangular attic window. Then join the others waiting on the wooden dock.

I packed you some supplies, Hesta says, handing us two cloth bags. I hope it will be enough.

I thank her and take her in my arms with gratitude and regret. Olio presses against my aunt's side.

Be careful, she repeats.

Diane and Boccus wish us good luck. Janot stands nearby. He hasn't prepared anything. His arms hang motionless at his sides. I give him a questioning look. He blushes and shakes his head.

Remember to bring me some books, he reminds Herman as my uncle sits down in the back of the canoe.

Olio studies Janot a moment then turns to the twins. Sylvia takes me in her arms and holds me. Darès steps forward. He shakes my hand, then tells me in a low voice to watch out, my young friend can do whatever he wants with me. I try not to show emotion but I can't help smiling when the twins start clowning around behind my uncle.

What are you two doing? he complains when he spots them each pressing one of his shoes to their ears.

Olio says it's like a seashell, Rémi and Roman explain in one voice, if you listen carefully you can hear the ocean.

Darès keeps his grumbling to himself. Hesta puts her hand on his shoulder to calm him down as Olio says goodbye to everyone but him, then jumps into the canoe.

I thank them all one at a time, carefully. Then, my throat tight, I take my place in the boat.

Herman dips the motor into the water. We untie the rope and Boccus pushes us off. The current slowly carries us away.

My family stands on the dock as if posing for a photo. With their angular faces marked by the sun and hard work, their patched hunting outfits, and their hair that has sprouted again, they look like sovereigns of another era at the borders of their kingdoms.

Suddenly I'm hesitating. What exactly am I doing? From the front, Olio turns in my direction. I envy his dazzling serenity.

Give Nep our regards, Darès jokes from the shore, his hands around his mouth to make his voice carry.

Herman looks away. He has had enough of his brother. He pulls on the starter cord. Accompanied by the irregular cough of the old outboard, we slip through the skeins of the net the giant trees have cast above our heads.

It dominates the world, pours down light, it is untouched by the shadows down here. Bristling with vanishing points, it is made of hopes, prayers, and unspoken tomorrows. The stories it has brought to life have never perished. No one has exhausted their meaning. God of ancient times or metal bird, it shelters everything that is out of reach. It oversees destinies, it lifts up hearts, it crushes bodies.

SKY

AFTERNOON

The river is wide and quiet. We follow its meandering for hours, lulled by the motor's low-speed grumble. Piled up in the bends are heaps of uprooted trees deposited by floods and the slow erosion of the current. The sandy banks are bordered by stands of pine hundreds of years old that hold fast to the ground until they give way in the unstoppable chaos of nature.

Olio leans forward in front like a figurehead. He glances back at me, victorious, ready for adventure. Jammed in between the boxes of supplies, I try to fathom what is happening. I have lost my watch. My family's calendar is far behind. We are going to the coast without knowing where we will end up. But the air is sweet, the afternoon flooded with sunshine, and the landscape takes over. My shoulders relax. I am seeing the forest for the first time.

I look back at Herman. His face is unreadable, one hand on the arm of the outboard and the other above his eyes to protect against the sun. When he manoeuvres to avoid a snag just below the surface, the wake of our changing path sends the sky's reflection wavering.

You know, my uncle begins, leaning towards me, when I took Nep with me last spring, he looked pretty much like you do. A lot of uncertainty in his eyes, but a shadow of relief all the same. What do you expect, that's family. I'm sure something is happening on the coast. Marchand will tell you. You can trust him.

Farther along, a few docks timidly reach into the sparkling body of the river. We can picture the camps behind the apparent tranquility of the trees. More people live in these parts. The flow is faster and carries us along, and we can feel the moving masses of water beneath the surface. Small waves whisper against the hull. Suddenly, the river widens out to form something like a lake: this is where two rivers come together. The currents meet and the canoe is tossed by the rippling water. Herman gives it gas and pilots us towards a quieter zone, into a bay. At the far end, a few buildings jut out from the side of the mountain. We move slowly towards a small metal dock where a rowboat is tied up. Herman cuts the engine.

There's someone there, he explains, we have to wait our turn. But we're lucky, sometimes there are a lot more people.

On both sides of the bay, among the rocks, I spot watchmen in lookout towers. A wooden fence runs along the bank and climbs towards the rocky heights. A metal gate opens onto a long stairway leading to sheds arranged like landings. Beyond the dull murmur of the rivers blending their water, bits of conversation reach us as two figures come down the stairs, loaded with sacks and boxes. A third man escorts them to the gate. Herman smiles.

That's Marchand.

The two men finish loading their rowboat and leave immediately. Herman waves to them politely, but they don't bother looking our way. They and their wake move off, accompanied by their sputtering engine. More people determined to remain ferociously alone in this world.

Marchand motions us to dock. Once we do, he puts out his hand to help Herman climb up, then greets him with a hug. Herman is by far the larger man, and Marchand disappears in his embrace.

On the door, a sign with big yellow letters.
Open.

I'm happy to see you, Herman, Marchand carries on, I was starting to get worried. And I see you haven't come alone.

My nephew and grandnephew, Herman says.

What are they doing here?

We're going to the coast, Olio immediately pipes up.

Yes, of course, he answers, pointing to one of the sheds higher up, but first let's start by unloading your stuff.

It takes us several round trips up and down the long stairway with our boxes, bags, and everything else we brought. After tying up our canoe around the back to keep it out of sight, Marchand invites us up. He padlocks the gate and turns the sign around.

Closed.

EVENING

In the shed, the shelves are lined with sacks of flour, rice, oats, and salt, and containers of oil. One of the walls is bursting with colour, preserves of all kinds, some homemade, others industrial. Amazed, Olio looks everywhere at once. Beets, meat, olives, peaches, hearts of palm, beans, pickled eggs.

Marchand evaluates the loot we have brought, taking a pencil out of his jacket.

That's a nice lot you have there, but there's a lot of fish and not much red meat.

We have what we have, Herman answers with a shrug. I'll tell you about it.

It's the same everywhere, Marchand agrees. Game is rare, so people are heading for the lakes.

My uncle pulls out his list.

We'll do that when it's time to go, Marchand interrupts him. You're here for a few days, I hope?

Herman looks embarrassed.

Come on, tell your family I needed help again, Marchand laughs. In the meantime, let's go to my place.

As we reach the next landing, the sound of barking has Olio and I on our guard. Next to a low building is a fenced-in yard containing four large, black dogs. Marchand whistles between his fingers to quiet them down, then opens the gate. The dogs rush to their master, sniff me, and lick Olio's hands. Marchand whistles a second time and the dogs run off. We climb another few steps up to a small house. His hideaway. A bedroom, kitchenette, and living room with shelves loaded with books. On one side, a table, a typewriter, piles of paper, scattered handwritten notes, an oil lamp, a soiled glass, an old dial telephone, a solar calculator, an ashtray overflowing with butts. Olio pushes on the typewriter keys and makes the carriage-return bell ring. He glances up, then picks up the receiver and dials a number. A few seconds of silence ensue, then Marchand suggests a drink on the deck outside. The view is magnificent. The two rivers battling over the same bed, the bay, and the forest that stretches out, green and moving, all the way to the rocky horizon line.

So you want to go to the coast? Marchand asks, sitting down. There are two ways to get there. If you go down the river, you'll need a good boat. There are whitewater rapids, quite the ride. But the people around the fishway are worse. They're keeping the salmon for themselves and blocking traffic. Let's just say they're not very accommodating.

Olio and I look at each other, dismayed.

Otherwise, you go through the woods. Do you have a map?

Olio searches through his bag and unfolds the map on the table. Marchand leans over the formless mass of gradient lines, then points out the junction of the two rivers: we are here. He moves his finger slowly eastward.

You'll first have to cross the burned section, he explains. Maybe you saw pictures on TV a few years back. The summer was very dry, and storms set off wildfires. Hundreds of square kilometres of forest turned to ash. Then you'll have to pass through peat bogs, cross the highlands, then go down to the lakes.

Then after, Olio insists, we'll reach the villages on the coast, right?

Marchand smiles at his determination.

What about the business with the wind turbines, I ask. Is it true?

Wind turbines! he scoffs. They're all along the coast. But plugging directly into one, I'm not sure, I've heard all kinds of talk. But you can say one thing, some villages are well organized. Where do you think the mead, the flour, the salt, and everything else comes from?

Night slowly surrounds us on the deck. The sky traces out the shape of the forest. A few crows caw from the treetops. Below, the fork of the rivers is a long arrow of shadow. Marchand goes on with his story.

One of my good friends had just left for the South when the blackout hit. I wonder what life is like these days under the palm trees. Here, everyone's scurrying around getting ready for winter, though most of them are completely overwhelmed by what's happening. Fresh air, pure water, life in the woods, that's what they dreamed of before all this happened.

Herman puts his hand on Marchand's shoulder. A quick current of tenderness passes between them. In the night, we hear the dogs frantically pacing the grounds. Above our heads, the heavens slowly drop their veil.

You see those three stars over there? Marchand goes on after a while. They make a line in the centre of a kind of square. The silhouette of a hunter with a knife in his belt. Look, there's an orange star on his left shoulder.

We try to pick out the constellation. He leans over to Herman to show him.

They say that one day, people put out his eyes and left him in the forest. After weeks of aimless wandering, a child came to him and climbed on his shoulders and guided him to the sea. And there, miraculously, he recovered his sight.

I try to picture Marchand's story in the pattern of the stars. The evening is quickly settling over me. A few glasses later, I fall asleep with Olio on the living-room sofa, listening to my uncle and his friend drink and talk until very late in the night.

When I open my eyes, the pink fingers of dawn are streaking the sky. Olio seems to have awakened sometime earlier. He is looking at the books that line the walls. Herman and Marchand join us later. We have something to eat, pick up our bags, and step outside. Marchand sends the dogs back behind their fence, then shakes our hands and shows us the way to reach the burned section. He considers us indulgently, wishes us luck, then goes down the long stairway to meet the watchmen who have come to take the day shift. In the trees, birds are singing their hearts out in hopes of drawing out the summer a little longer.

Some leave and some stay, Herman says, holding back his feelings. That's the way it is. To each his burden.

Olio steps forward to say goodbye. My uncle takes his face between his thick hands and kisses him on the top of his head. Then looks to me.

Don't you have a rifle? Wait there, I'll give you mine.

Not necessary. It's too heavy for no reason. Hesta gave us a lot of supplies.

Maybe, my uncle answers, but it's always useful, and you know it.

We made it to the camp without a weapon. We should be able to reach the coast the same way.

Herman gazes at me, his eyes full, then takes me in his arms. I let his strength and warmth wrap around me.

Take good care of your boy, he whispers in my ear. Then he backs away, turns on his heel, and runs down the stairs after Marchand.

Once he has gone, Olio and I move back into the woods, towards our new destination. Olio is impatient. But I fear what will come next, because with each step, the chance to change our minds grows dimmer.

MIDDAY

We walk through blueberry barrens, birch saplings, blackened stumps, and trunks stripped by the burn. Slowly I relearn how to handle the weight of my pack. My knee is holding up. Marchand warned us. There is no trail, no road, no infrastructure anywhere in the sector. Our eyes are our only guide. My hands on my sticks, I move along behind Olio, who easily finds his way through the bush. From time to time, I make him stop so we can get oriented.

In the evening, we camp out under the tarp. The nights are getting cold. If I don't wake up to feed the fire, the dew settles on us and turns to frost in the wee hours. During the day, winter's reminder seems unreal. We travel through this desolate stretch. It is hot, the sun draws a great arc above our heads, and with every step, charred branches crumble beneath our feet. We come upon a hawk perched on the branch of a blackened tree. It looks at us with irritation, spreads its wings, and disappears into the air like a tawny arrow. Later, Olio spots the entrance to a den under a heap of tangled roots. Home to a bear, probably. I object, but he goes inside to have a look. For a second I am afraid that a black shape will emerge, its heavy arms around Olio. Nothing of the sort happens. I pull him out of there and scold him for his recklessness. He cares nothing for my opinion and stares absent-mindedly at the horizon of this charred landscape and the humped back of the highlands beyond.

AFTERNOON

We make our way through the peat bogs, and it is tough going. We have to sidestep the swampy parts with their oily circles and decomposing cattails and roots. Like tightrope walkers, we balance on the narrow, grassy bands that offer passage through the muck. Here and there are foreshortened trunks. They stand like grey figures, marble statues, the last pillars of a ruined world.

We take a break to figure out where we are. Side by side on a little rise, we chew on a piece of smoked turkey. The texture is good and it is perfectly salted. The comforting taste of meat reminds me of my family, their knowledge and discipline, their domain.

Fat, insistent flies circle us. Olio points out a red, trumpet-shaped flower, one of many.

Look, the flies that crawl into it never come out. The flower eats them.

He leans over for a closer look. His bag tips over and a revolver drops onto the yellow grass.

What are you doing with that?

It's a souvenir from Marchand's, he tells me. I found it in the room where he and Herman slept, in the drawer of the bedside table.

You call that a souvenir? I say, exasperated. You're going to get caught one day. And when that happens, don't count on me to defend you.

He gets mad when I slip the gun into my pack. He's upset,

I have no right, it's his, he knows how to use it. I'm just as hard-headed as my uncle Darès.

I want nothing more than to slap him across the face. My nerves jump and strain. He stares at me, ready for anything, and when I make no move, he picks up his bag and goes off. I cast my eyes on this humid, inhospitable land. A cloud bank covers the horizon. I wonder what I've gotten myself into. And what to expect from the place we're going. And, most of all, what this stubborn kid I'm trying to tame wants. A heron moves among the lily pads nearby without paying me the slightest attention.

When I stand up, my knee buckles and I lose my balance on a tuft of grass. My foot slips into the swampy water. With the suction, I have to fight to free my leg. I curse. The heron flies off. A fetid odour follows me as I take to the road beneath the dark cloak of the sky.

MID-MORNING

The rain started as soon as we reached higher elevations. Every evening, we try to dry our clothes by the fire, but it is impossible to get rid of the foul humidity.

    We zigzag along a slope besieged by clouds. The higher we climb, the more trees there are and the tighter their net. I slip through the openings between bushes and stands of pine. The branches grab onto my clothes and my pack. I call to Olio several times, ordering him to wait for me. Stubbornly, I attack the steep grades, fighting off the underbrush of small conifers that want to hold me back. I remember the fly in the trumpet-shaped carnivorous flower as I struggle to pull myself free. I am in tatters and gasping for breath when I finally catch up to Olio on a rocky outcrop. He chuckles at the state I'm in and we head out again through the mist, following an exposed ridge. We can hardly see anything. Rocks roll away beneath our feet into invisible precipices. I move forward carefully to keep from slipping while Olio hums a tune up ahead, at one with the fog.

    The rain finally stops and the wind blows away the cloud cover. We are on one of the round peaks of the highlands, surrounded by low bushes clinging to the ground with unshakeable will. On one side, we can see the great reddish plane of the peat bogs that fade into the ashen immensity of the burned section. On the other, lakes beyond counting. Even if we can't see it yet, I breathe in deeply, hoping to sense the salty air of the coast.

We ease our way down the other side of the highlands and reach the depths of the forest by the end of the day. We bypass a number of lakes, trying to stay on course with the compass. Night soon settles in, but Olio refuses to stop. He convinces me to go a little farther using the headlamp. I follow the narrow skein of light that cuts through the darkness. I fall behind; I'm completely wiped out.

It's late. Let's find a place.

No, Olio tells me. Not here.

Darkness envelops me as he walks away, jumping over fallen trunks. I have had enough. I raise my voice.

All right already! You stop right now!

To my surprise, he obeys. I hurry after him, figuring he has found a camping spot. I catch up, then stop stock-still. Besides the poplar trees whispering in the wind, the forest is dead quiet. Between two bramble bushes, in the headlamp, stands a tall, grey shape with piercing yellow eyes. A wolf. It can't be the only one.

I whisper to Olio, we'd better move on. He ignores me and creeps forward. I'm in a rage – please don't be an idiot. The wolf retreats a few steps when it sees the boy coming at him, and watches him go by, pivoting its head slightly. I can't believe my eyes. But as soon as Olio has his back turned, a yellow flash splits the night. The wolf leaps on him. I shout and attack the animal with my sticks. My knee gives way and I end up on the ground. Two more wolves emerge from the darkness. We are surrounded. Olio mutters something. The gun. Keeping my eyes on the wolves watching me, I pull myself over to my pack, grab the revolver, and shoot over their heads.

The gunshot shakes the forest. The wolves freeze, smell the scent of gunpowder, then retreat into the shadow world.

NIGHT

Olio gets to his feet. His composure is otherworldly. But his face is white.

I'll be all right, he says, adjusting his headlamp. There's nothing wrong.

He is lying. He was bitten on the ankle. My hands tremble as I examine the wound. It doesn't look too bad. The traces of two fangs. Two small black holes that pierce his skin. Like a snakebite. I disinfect the area with alcohol pads and wrap his ankle in gauze.

We set up camp farther on, between a rock wall and a boggy pond. I keep the fire burning all night and watch anxiously over the darkness. I picture the scene over and over again. Olio creeping closer. The wolf retreating, then waiting to spring. I should have reacted quicker. I should have held Olio back. I should have kept the gun close at hand.

The next morning, a red circle radiates out from Olio's wound. He grimaces when he tries to move his foot. He is going to have trouble walking. We stare at the branches bending over the silty banks of the pond and say nothing. I think of the supplies in my pack. We are in good shape. We could easily take a few days off to rest.

No way, he replies, getting to his feet. His easy movements are a performance for my behalf. If we want to get to the coast, we'd better move.

EVENING

Limping, Olio leans on the two sticks I found for him. My knee is not doing so well, either. A couple of walking wounded. We push on through the day, then give in to fatigue and make camp under the boughs of a stand of young cedar.

I take off Olio's shoe and pull away the gauze. Swelling has set in from heel to calf. I hide how worried I am. But I know what's coming. We are going to have to get him some antibiotics.

We eat hazelnuts and pheasant preserved in its fat. Delicious. Olio declares that he's all better now. He takes out the map and locates the coastal villages with a dreamy look.

That evening, my little guy falls asleep nestled against me. His breathing is choppy. The coals of the fire speak in low voices. This is the hour when the forest changes its face. The rough hoot of a screech owl breaks the silence. Clouds chase each other noiselessly, like a herd of worried creatures. I decide to go look for more wood, then change my mind and stay with Olio, hoping to protect him from the talons of the night.

MORNING

The next morning, Olio can hardly move. He pushes off heavily on his sticks with small, leaping steps. I close my eyes a moment and breathe in. Then what I do next is faster and more efficient, though I know there is no way out of this forest.

I empty my pack on the ground and sort through our supplies, keeping only part of them. Olio looks on with no idea what I am doing. Dark circles have bloomed under his eyes. I strap my pack to my chest, kneel down, and tell him to climb on my back. I stand up, grab my sticks, lean my body forward, and take off, trying to see where my next step is leading me.

For the first part of the morning, Olio manages to hang on, and though my knee is painful, we move along nicely. His chin rests on my shoulder. I feel his breath on my ear.

You know, he murmurs, I don't lie and I don't steal. I just do what I can to get out of the woods. I see the towns on the coast with their turbines and the houses all lit up at night. I know you're sad because we left your family. But I don't need anyone. Except you.

His voice is weak, and as we move along, his head rolls from side to side, his hands lose their grip, and his arms slide down my body. I squat down and sit him on a carpet of ferns.

He says he's cold. I want to hold him, but he tips over on his side. The effect of his fever. I examine his ankle. The swelling and redness reach up to his thigh. The bite marks are hardly visible on his swollen leg. I throw my head back. I am helpless, I need a phone booth, a cab, the front door of a hospital. The wind toys with the tall grass and stirs me from lethargy. I find two long branches and build a makeshift stretcher with my tarp and some rope. I place Olio in the middle and give him water. It runs down his chin. He is shivering. I wrap him in his survival blanket, take hold of the stretcher, and drag him across the thick humus of the forest floor. He moans when we get stuck on a stump or a rock. I tell him, hang on tight, trust me, and haul him along, sweating, breathing hard in my flight forward.

AFTERNOON

We come to a lake. It's big and I'm discouraged when I think we'll have to walk our way around it tomorrow. I set down the stretcher, my strength completely gone. My knee wants to explode. Behind a line of cattails is a pebbly beach. I settle Olio as comfortably as I can on the shore and gather firewood. He protests a little, but his breathing seems more stable.

The wind is calm. The smoke rises into the clear sky. High above us is a thin crescent moon, white and pale. I lean over my companion. His hands are sweaty and his cheeks boiling. He opens his eyes when he feels me near.

Don't let go, I tell him, pressing my forehead to his, stay with me. I'll find some way out of this. Until then, save your strength, sleep, I'll wake you tomorrow when it's time.

The crackling fire slices through the silence. Daylight slowly fades. The lake is a deep mirror. When the first stars show themselves, the forest becomes a dotted line between two crystal worlds.

Besides pushing on, I don't know what we can do. We're alone in the world and Olio needs medication. We shouldn't have left the camp.

A distant buzzing sound attracts my attention. It grows louder, coming our way. I stand up. The noise a prop plane makes. On the edges of the evening, it appears above the highlands. Position lights blink from its wings. The motor's output is uneven. The plane nears us, its engine coughing.

It lines up its approach to the lake, then hits the water hard. Its pontoons send up a powerful spray.

I stand on the bank, completely at a loss. Waves break at my feet. I can hardly believe what I'm seeing.

TWILIGHT

I pick up Olio's silver blanket and wave it high in the air. The float plane gently slips towards our position. The motor is sputtering, then it cuts out. Trouble. The propeller comes to a halt. I tuck in Olio again and tell him to hang on, then throw a good handful of wood on the fire. We are saved.

A door opens in the thin cylinder of yellow metal. Two figures step out. A man and a woman. They look around, greet us with a nod. They talk to each other in another language. Then the man speaks to me in a strong accent. He wants to know if the boy is all right.

He was bitten, I say immediately, he needs antibiotics. Please take us with you.

I'm afraid we have engine trouble, he tells me.

I'm a mechanic.

He translates for his friend. She looks me over, eyes wide, then speaks one short sentence.

She says we should be able to work something out.

Quickly, my voice broken with emotion, I ask them where they are going.

The coast. Less than an hour's flight.

Night stretches out across the lake. The two friends move towards the fire, chewing on a protein bar.

You heard them, I say to Olio, we're going to fly to the coast.

He is sleeping, stirring from time to time when he coughs up phlegm. The woman looks concerned. I point at the float plane and tell them I want to start right away. The woman nods and the man quickly takes a toolbox and a flashlight from the plane.

My entire being is absorbed by the task. There's no time to lose. Olio won't last forever. I open the panels that enclose the propeller shaft, then look at the overall shape of the engine. The faded yellow of the cockpit and the algae stuck to the pontoons make me think the craft has not been used for a while. I inspect the motor. An old model with big pistons in a circular formation.

It's bad-quality gas, I deduce. Like everywhere else. We can always clean the injection system. It can't hurt.

The man translates for the woman. She motions me to go ahead and holds the flashlight close, watching my every move. I detach the hose assembly, unscrew the brackets, loosen up a part that was blocking the flow, and manage to ease out the fuel pump. I hand it to the woman, who holds it in her hands like a beating heart.

We sit on a large, flat rock under the weakening beam of the flashlight and take apart the pump, piece by piece. We rub and clean each one with the remains of a lubricant spray found in the plane. When the time comes to put the pump back together, a piece is missing. We search around the rock. We turn out our pockets. Nothing. I panic. Without that little metal part, we're going nowhere.

Miraculously, the woman finds it among the pebbles on the shore. More than relieved, I install the part, tighten the bolts, and put the pump back where it belongs, in the inner workings of the engine. Behind us, to the east, the starry sky is beginning to give way to daybreak.

DAWN

I feed the fire to keep the morning chill off Olio. As soon as the sun rises, the woman settles in at the controls and tests the engine. It roars, coughs, belches, then miraculously begins purring smoothly.

The woman leans against the plane's windshield and gives us the thumbs-up.

Let's go, the man says behind me, time to move.

I run to Olio and gather him up in my arms. Hold on, in an hour we'll be on the coast. I'm sure we'll find antibiotics. But Olio is unconscious. His clothes are soaked with cold sweat and his muscles are limp. I might as well be carrying a puppet without strings. I limp as fast as I can towards the plane. The sun casts my shadow on the shore, but strangely I don't see Olio's limbs sticking out on both sides, as if the light flowed right through them. I place him in the plane as carefully as I can. The inside is smaller than it looks. I manage to settle him in without his leg banging into anything. The two travellers are shocked when they see his ashen face and empty eyes. They exchange a questioning look and put on their earphones.

A moment later, the whole plane vibrates as we pull away from the shore. I see the empty stretcher and the smoky fire. The pilot gives it gas, the propeller blades push through the air, and we are drawn forward. Through the window, the trees rush past. I hold Olio's frozen hands tightly. The engine strains. We accelerate, but without taking off. Then the nose of the plane points skyward, the pontoons pull away from the lake, and we just manage to avoid the wall of trees in front of us.

We are airborne. The plane makes a wide turn as it gains altitude. Below, the forest is a thin carpet of bas-relief dotted with countless shining lakes.

I feel my body relax as we climb. I even think I see Olio's bluish lips turn upward in a smile.

A slight variation in the engine's hum catches my ear. I listen closely. Probably just a reaction to a change in atmospheric pressure.

The pilot's eyes move across the indicators on the dashboard panel. Our seats shake with every bump and our little metal bird casts a graceful shadow on the fabric of the forest.

The landscape stretches out beneath us like a topographical map. We cross the sky, drawing daylight with us. I am in wonderment: the sight I never hoped for, that I could not have expected. Olio is lifeless. His waxy skin does not belong to him. A trail of saliva runs down the sides of his mouth. I look at him but refuse to see. I kiss him. Embrace him. Hold him close. In a panic. He has to keep fighting. We're almost there. Without the light of his eyes, I am nothing. He is my destination.

The plane is shaking harder. I'm worried. I picture all the parts of the fuel pump that we disassembled, cleaned, then put back. It can't be that.

I try to warn the pilot, but the racket of the engine drowns out my voice and sinks my heart.

I glance out the window. Unbelievable, the blue line of the water in the distance, bordered by valleys dotted with wind turbines. I shake Olio so he can see it, too, but his body slumps forward. I catch him just in time. The engine coughs heavily. It chokes and goes silent. The pilot and the man sit petrified in their seats. The only sound is the air whistling over the fragile metal fuselage. The propeller stops turning. The plane glides between forest and sky, losing altitude.

And I hold my son close with all the strength I have.

ACKNOWLEDGMENTS

The author would like to thank the Canada Council for the Arts and the Conseil des arts et des lettres du Québec as well as Mylène Bouchard, Simon Philippe Turcot, Paul Kawzack, Brigitte Caron, Antoine Joie, Nicolas Rochette, François Lamarche, Lisa Liautaud, Hugette Guay, Réjean Guay, Nicole Guay, Alain Guay, Michel Guay, Michel Genest, Pauline Mulin, Maude-Hélène Desroches, Véronique de Broin, Diane Cormier, Jonathan Cormier, Josée Beaudet, and Lucie Dumont.

DAVID HOMEL is the author of fifteen novels. As a translator, he has twice won the Governor General's Award. He lives in Montréal.

PHOTO BY MARINA VULICEVIC

CHRISTIAN GUAY-POLIQUIN was born back when the environmental stakes were limited to a hole in the ozone and acid rain. Though his books refer to the codes of post-apocalyptic fiction, their ambition is not to tell another end-of-the-world story. Instead, they bring us face to face with the strengths and fragile quality of human relations. His novels *Running on Fumes* (2013) and *The Weight of Snow* (2016), winner of the Governor General's Literary Award for French-Language Fiction, have been published in several languages around the world.

PHOTO BY LAURENCE GRANDBOIS-BERNARD